THE NINTH WAVE

For my children, Rebecca, Ben and Rachel, with love. Wales is in you too.

RUSSELL CELYN JONES
THE NINTH WAVE

NEW STORIES FROM THE
MABINOGION

Russell Celyn Jones

SEREN

Seren is the book imprint of
Poetry Wales Press Ltd
57 Nolton Street, Bridgend, Wales, CF31 3AE
www.seren-books.com

ISBN 978-1-85411-514-0

A CIP record for this title is available from the British Library.

Cover design by Mathew Bevan

Inner design and typesetting by books@lloydrobson.com

Printed in the Czech Republic by Akcent Media Ltd

The publisher acknowledges the financial support of the
Welsh Books Council.

New Stories from the Mabinogion

Introduction

Some stories, it seems, just keep on going. Whatever you do to them, the words are still whispered abroad, a whistle in the reeds, a bird's song in your ear.

Every culture has its myths; many share ingredients with each other. Stir the pot, retell the tale and you draw out something new, a new flavour, a new meaning maybe. There's no one right version. Perhaps it's because myths were a way of describing our place in the world, of putting people and their search for meaning in a bigger picture that they linger in our imagination.

The eleven stories of the *Mabinogion* ('story of youth') are diverse native Welsh tales taken from two medieval manuscripts. But their roots go back hundreds of years, through written fragments and the unwritten, storytelling tradition. They were first collected under this title, and translated into English, in the nineteenth century.

The *Mabinogion* brings us Celtic mythology, Arthurian romance, and a history of the Island of Britain seen through the eyes of medieval Wales – but tells tales that stretch way beyond the boundaries of contemporary Wales, just as the 'Welsh' part of this island once did: Welsh was once spoken as far north as Edinburgh. In one tale, the gigantic Bendigeidfran wears the crown of London, and his severed head is buried there, facing France, to protect the land from invaders.

There is enchantment and shape-shifting, conflict, peacemaking, love, betrayal. A wife conjured out of flowers is punished for unfaithfulness by being turned into an owl, Arthur and his knights chase a magical wild boar and its piglets from Ireland across south Wales to Cornwall, a prince changes places with the king of the underworld for a year...

Many of these myths are familiar in Wales, and some have filtered through into the wider British tradition, but others are little known beyond the Welsh border. In this series of New Stories from the Mabinogion the old tales are at the heart of the new, to be enjoyed wherever they are read.

Each author has chosen a story to reinvent and retell for their own reasons and in their own way: creating fresh, contemporary tales that speak to us as much of the world we know now as of times long gone.

Penny Thomas, series editor

The Ninth Wave

One

He came back from war to find his own land had grown remote. Six months away was all it took. Now a cold mist was rising sluggishly from the lakes. White frost hung on branches. Fields welded with grey skies. And he felt indifferent. Viewed from horseback, the landscape reneged on him. It failed to revive his spirits. With him rode a dozen men, all paid-up hunting companions whose names he barely knew.

He was missing his time in the army, at the front-line in the south-west. He'd been an officer – by privilege of his birth admittedly. Everyone understood the NCOs were his superiors really, but no one spoke of it. Older men conditioned by war, they'd taught him to control muscle-racking fear by breathing in steam; how, in hand-to-hand fighting, the best method for overpowering the enemy was to stamp on his foot. To be a good soldier you had to be a canny one.

He led the hunting party along railway sleepers laid over a hoary ground. Every now and then he caught a glimpse of the necklace of industries around the throat of the bay – producing little more than memories now – and the lamb-white beaches stretching further west. Out at sea, cargo ships were slinging in from Yokohama, Shanghai; all those places. Rio, Cape Town. Their huge white sails flopped and mooned and inhaled the wind. Clouds in the distance played upon the surface of the water, changing from white to pink and green to a rich aubergine.

Since oil ran out, warfare had become medieval again. Armies now breached city barricades with battering rams, or scaled them with ladders while defenders poured boiling water upon their heads (pitch could only be dreamed of). Advanced military technology lay rusting in the grass for want of a gallon of diesel. You could no longer call in air. Ground troops charged enemy lines on horseback. They laced their steeds' feed buckets with Afghan poppy before riding like the wind into a contact, or away from a lost one. With no high-tech it was scary shit again; hand-to-hand fighting with the Moroccans who came by sea on sail-driven frigates, and once on land were powerful by virtue of some vintage stocks of crude. Enough to run a single tank at least, and a single tank nowadays could turn the tide of a war.

He hoped he'd killed some of those Moroccans personally, but couldn't bank on it. He was protected by his men, who did the killing for him, while he had to contend with putting down 5.56mm GPMG fire from a safe distance, covering his platoon who rode their stoned fillies on short violent pilgrimages across enemy lines. They always returned minus one of the men he called uncle.

If truth be told he was scared of violence. That's what he learned about himself during his short stint in the military. And in that game if you didn't love violence, no one would love you. He hid it the best he could, slaughtering a lamb each night to feed his platoon. Cooking with the guys in a darkened field after a rout – that was what he lived for. Sitting around a roaring fire, swearing with them, hearing accounts of their kills. In the army you could say what you liked. There was no control over their statements, or his. He could be as indiscreet as they were.

He'd been removed from the front when the contacts got too hot. He was never in any real danger the whole time. Those men would have protected him with their lives. Granted they'd been ordered to, but he hoped some of them had got to love him just a little bit by the end of his tour.

The land up here was scraped clean by prevailing south-westerly winds. High enough to see the sea at all times, but not the deer. Now noon, and the temperature had soared, burning off the mists. It often reached 29°C in mid-September. Seasons were so arbitrary nowadays, as was the time of day – at least to Pwyll, who didn't work, didn't wake up until he felt like it. Another hour passed and they reached the woods and expectation grew. They dismounted to be low to the mossy floor. Above them pigeons fled the treetops in panic, rattling their bony wings against the topmost branches. A flurry of dust fell down through the shafts of light.

He began to smell a sweet scent of flowers on the air. Only good things should come from such olfactory places. While holding this thought, he led the men into a clearing where the sun broke through and where old cars, with tyres burnt off and engines removed, had been stuffed with compost and manure – for the cultivation of hothouse flowers: the bi-coloured Soleil D'Or and the Grand Monarch from China. Apache horticulturalists lived in the other cars and sold the blooms for a living.

Teirnon, his steward, who'd served under his father, moved his horse up the line to walk beside Pwyll.

'How's your lordship doing?' he asked brightly.

'To be truthful, Teirnon, fucking bored to death.'

'On such a grand day as this?' His thin lips opening into a smile revealed baby-sized teeth.

Teirnon was in his late forties and that he could still enjoy a hunt confounded Pwyll, who was twenty-four. 'Why are we hunting anyway, when Sainsbury's wraps it all up for us?'

Teirnon stared at him indulgently. Pwyll knew his steward would be judging now which was the best way to reply. His job depended on having the right hunch. And he'd been in that job a long time. In the end he said nothing and that was about right.

Earlier that day they'd ridden past isolated farm-houses and through villages. People came out onto the road to pay tribute to Lord Pwyll – but out of duty, not love; not even for a warrior back from the front. They knew he'd been sent to war as a PR exercise. The fake pride showed in their upturned faces. He sneered back at them from the saddle, staring down teenage girls' cleavages to irritate their fathers.

The gamekeepers, cooks, gardeners, stable boys, carpenters and plumbers riding with him were similarly dutiful, rounded up from off the estate by an ever-cautious Teirnon. Pwyll pulled the reins down hard to let his horse graze on clover and walked off into the woods in a strop. Soldiers, they were the best of men, the only real people in his life, who kept it honest for him.

'If you wish, my lord,' Teirnon said, catching up, 'we can turn back for the house.'

'No, no, forget that.' The hunt was all there was. 'We'll get a kill first.'

But the herd was proving elusive. They moved on and reached the old slate quarry without sighting a single deer. Here the mountainside had been carved into terraces by a previous generation, exposing its blue, green and purple belly to the light for the first time in millions of years. Below these terraces was a lake pigmented a turquoise blue. The lake had been one of his regular haunts since he was a kid, a place where he could be alone with his thoughts. In more recent times old cookers, freezers and washing machines had been dumped there and broke the surface of the water. A dark blue Nissan perched at the lake's edge. He could see its deep tracks in the mud. It was still in relatively good condition even without its tyres. From the back fender dangled a severed orange rope. In the windscreen were two bullet holes.

He dismounted, wandered over to the car and opened the passenger door. On the driver's side were Order of Service cards for a marriage ceremony. *Sinead and Vaughan, at Clare Vale church.* Either a bygone wedding or one the bride and groom had never reached. With these wedding cards in hand he meditated on the silent domestic appliances in the lake. Along the shore, willows had collapsed into the water. The light felt almost frail and he could hear the sound of a river fading, losing power, unable to reach its final destination of the sea.

He strayed far from the party. He allowed his horse to follow but not the men. From the edge of the lake he saw fish jumping, struggling to leave their watery prison. A single swan sat on the turquoise water. It too seemed between places, away from home, confused. A breeze skimmed the surface, making ripples. The metallic sound of leaves rustling, a smell of cut pine. Noises of animals being preyed upon. Airborne attacks on rats and voles...

He threw a rock into the lake to stimulate something, make something move. He watched the concentric circles expand until they reached his feet. Distant sounds of sheep and cattle, dogs barking from afar. Lots of different birds flying by: murder of crows, pairs of jays and magpies, songbirds singing their hearts out in fear of the jays and magpies.

Fifty metres away, his men waited patiently for him to give directions.

He felt the sun burn his face. He heard the fish clatter and rattle as they swam amongst the submerged fridges, cookers and tumble-driers. Married couples dumped their wares here. That swan! Pearl-white with a dirty neck, head in the water, tail in the air.

On the crest of the hill appeared a stag – a glorious, grey muscle-bound alpha male etched upon the skyline. Pwyll felt his heart pull and dive. He sensed the men flinch, saw their arms reach out very slowly for holstered weapons hanging from saddles. They had a clear shot from here, but no one would go before him.

A sound of slate shards clicking; the deer turned its beautiful neck. Pwyll heard the dog before he saw it – a bark like a violently snapped branch. A brown-freckled ridgeback came off the ground at speed, drooling and snarling, and fell upon the stag, engorging itself. The stag screamed. The scream had no end and was heartbreaking to hear.

The way into this was clear in his mind. He unsheathed his Finnish bolt-action rifle from the saddle and began running along the rim of the lake. He jumped from one boulder to another. When he was high enough to see the dog's spine protruding through its skin, he braced himself with legs apart, drew the bolt, took aim and shot it through the neck. It fell upon the stag, both animals trembling. The stag scrambled from beneath the weight of the dog, got unsteadily to its legs, briefly looked around at the world. It seemed to wait for some kind of confirmation. Then it leapt away, flying the arterial red flag.

Pwyll stood with his boot on the throat of the ridgeback – a huge and frightening dog, even when dead. From over an escarpment another hunting party appeared. They had come from the east, on Arab horses, five men in black North Face jackets. One of these men broke from the group. He stemmed his mount into a slow trot as soon as he saw the dog, and slid down from the saddle. Pwyll stepped away, holding his weapon across his waist, parallel to the ground. Teirnon caught up with him and they both watched this other man fall to his knees over the dog. Then they heard him exhale.

He pulled the dog's limp head into his chest, kissed it and then let it crash to the ground. Rising to his full height he glowered at Pwyll, saying nothing. He had bad skin, the ravages of teenage acne. His eyes were remote and bloodshot.

Pwyll broke the silence, giving the other man the advantage. 'Your dog was attacking the stag.'

'Well, it's called hunting. Isn't that what you're doing?'

'Not with dogs.'

The stranger threw back his head in the direction of his men, who all looked sprung from the same caged womb, with the same buzz haircuts, square jaws. 'I don't accept your apologies.'

'I didn't apologise,' Pwyll said.

The man caressed the neck of his horse and lowered his voice to a hiss. 'You're the young bard of war, aren't you? The one they sent away because you were misspending your youth with people you shouldn't know.'

'You have the advantage, sir.'

Teirnon interrupted, translating the unspoken line. 'This is Lord Arawn. He has the land east of the river.'

'Arawn?' Pwyll repeated. He did not know the name.

The man's hand that was stroking the horse was covered in hair, his nails broken and dirty; an aristocrat with the hands of a gravedigger. 'How are we going to do this, son?'

'You want compensation?' Pwyll struggled to keep his voice from breaking.

'No, son, that cock won't crow.' His remark drew a snigger from his men. Pwyll noticed their easy familiarity and envied it. They slid off their horses and lifted the dead animal onto one of the saddles and mounted up again. Without another word all of them set off, riding slowly towards the escarpment from which they'd emerged.

Pwyll was shaking. He wanted to fall into someone's arms. He said to Teirnon, 'Why should he be pissed off with *me* for shooting his dog?'

'Arawn's a man of reckless determination.'

'Did you see their jackets? Gortex is hard to come by.'

'Arawn looks after his men – that is true.' He gravely lowered his voice. 'Be warned, this is not over.'

Their hunt was now completely ruined and everyone knew it. The party headed back to the estate as the weather changed. They rode through the sodden woods under dripping trees onto the highway, as a way of making time. Each carriageway was lined with cars refitted for human habitation. People who lived in them had grown Veronica as windbreaks, a few stiff Monterey pines from California. Pwyll liked being on this road. Fluttering around the cracked wing mirrors of a VW van were blue tits trying to mate with their own image.

This way back skirted the Sandfields housing estate. He knew this scruffy tip was where Teirnon hailed from and could feel the steward's dis-ease as they rode into it. At its heart was a biomass power station that burned 500,000 tons of clean woodchip each year, producing high pressure steam to turn the turbines, generating 50MW in renewable electricity. Pwyll could still remember a time when a petro-chemical plant had stood in its place. Then a small boy, his father brought him out here to teach him about industry. From anywhere on the estate in those days you could hear chemicals humming under hot recycle in the knotted steel pipes, see twenty-foot heads of flame issuing from the plant's stack. A river was diverted into the plant so ships could sail right in and have their holds pumped full of benzene and vinyl chloride monomer. That was some tough era. At night the plant was a mass of white light and steam, actually quite beautiful. But to see things in this way, in the electric green with a metallic wind in your hair, is what it means to be young. Now his thoughts were turned to more tormenting things – the unarticulated threat posed by Arawn – and that's what it means to grow old.

They rode past weaving and embroidery factories, a John Deere tractor workshop (defunct), trailer park, units making bathroom tiles, bamboo flooring. Each street was named after a famous composer. Gangs of teenagers walked their pit bulls down Mozart Avenue towards the War Memorial and acknowledged Pwyll like they would the police. Since his father and mother died, powers had been invested in him. He was meant to rule here but didn't know how. He had yet to inspire any affection.

He asked Teirnon breezily, 'You still have family here?'

'Only one brother now.'

This sounded fine to Pwyll, one brother was one more than he had. Why it cost Teirnon to say so, was hard to understand. 'I want to visit your brother,' he announced.

'You want to visit my brother?' Teirnon repeated.

Pwyll could tell his idea didn't appeal.

'That's what I said.' He did not stop to consider the consequence to Teirnon or his brother of making such an impromptu visit.

Dutifully, Teirnon took him to a row of faded grey houses. They left their horses and walked up one of the garden paths. Pwyll could feel his steward's resentment in the mute shuffle. 'It's no big deal,' he reassured him, 'just a little social visit.' The front lawn was nibbled to the stub. Something hungry had this way passed.

They reached the door, rang the bell and a shadow behind the frosted glass panel began to move. The door swung open and standing before them was a stooped old man with fine grey hair matted with dust. There was dirt in his ears and rimming his nostrils. If he wasn't overjoyed to see his brother and his lord, he tried not to show it. He stretched his arm behind his back, gesturing them to enter.

From the street, the windows were badly smeared so Pwyll got no forewarning of what lay inside. As he stepped over the threshold the smell made him gag. Then he saw the horse in the living room. It appeared to be out on its legs, head drooping. Surrounding this world-weary nag were cabinets stuffed with bone china and silverware.

The man didn't so much as mention the horse. He repaired to the kitchen, which smelled different but not much sweeter. There was a thick layer of grease on every surface and Pwyll's soles stuck to the floor.

'Tea?' the brother offered, dragging the syllable out like a wet rag.

As the kettle boiled, he plucked three festering mugs from the sink of dirty crockery and gave them a quick rinse. Since no one else was talking, Pwyll questioned him about the mare in the front room.

'Why isn't she grazing outside?'

The brother's face soured and scrunched up. 'She'll get cancer, all the carcinogens in the air.'

'Do you ride her?' Pwyll asked.

'I have a little sideline as a rag and bone merchant, your lordship.'

Teirnon said, 'She'd make you more money as carcase for dog food. You'd earn more from her dead

27

than alive. Either that or she should be out on the moors, eating clover and grass in her final days.' He sounded bitter and angry. This was not the demon-stration of brotherly love Pwyll had hoped to find.

'Carcinogens reach to the moors too,' his brother said.

'How so?' Pwyll asked.

'From Havgan's plant.'

The name was not familiar to Pwyll. 'What plant is this?'

'Emissions from that plant eat the paintwork off my windows. Lacquer smell's been coming into my lavatory, through the sewerage system.'

The brother poured hot water over the tea bags and dribbled evaporated milk from a can into the mugs. They sat in silence for a while longer before he got up from the table to go feed his mare. Pwyll watched him lean into the horse's backside while emptying a saucepan of grain into a feed bucket. There were huge dents in the walls from where the horse had kicked back with its hind legs.

Teirnon was looking desperately humiliated. This

visit was undermining the impression he liked to give of a man from nowhere, who'd parented himself.

All that he was learning today left Pwyll feeling weightless. He drifted to his feet and made their excuses, to set Teirnon free of the past. On the way out, he stalled at the bathroom door. He needed to go, but once he'd pushed open the door and looked in, thought better of it. Some scenes are best left undescribed.

Pwyll's own home was a thirty-five-roomed mansion on 1000 acres of prime farmland. Men harvesting wheat looked up as the hunting party rode in. Once maintained by a few large machines, the farm was now pecked over by teams using hand tools – men who he rarely met. He knew nothing about farming and didn't care to learn.

In the courtyard, he slid out of the saddle and wrapped the reins around a stable boy's raised arm. After entering the house by the hall he sluggishly climbed the double staircase, past portraits of his dead ancestors.

From the landing he was lured into his parents' bedroom. Months after their deaths and it still smelled of oysters, which for some reason he always associated with nuns. His mother had been a believer and her rosary beads were draped over the corner bedpost. Pontormo's painting of the Deposition hung on the wall. After their deaths he gave orders to the cleaning staff that nothing in this room be changed. A few blouses hung from wire hangers on the picture rail. White jeans were folded on a chair and the last book his father had read lay open with its spine broken. On a bedside table were a beeswax candle and a Kodak envelope of photographs.

He sat on the edge of the bed and flicked through the photographs, holding up to the sunset the picture of his mother as a young bride on a swing; his father in Royal Welch Fusiliers uniform. This was his favourite. They had died six months apart.

His own bedroom had altered very little either. He kept the curtains drawn. On the wall behind his bed was a collage he'd made as an angry teenager from magazine pictures realigned in ways you don't see in

Vogue. Models were burning in furnaces in a city of erect penises. Men were cars from the waist down... auto centaurs. A fierce orange sun was painted into the top left-hand corner around the light switch.

No one but his parents and the cleaners had seen this collage, which is more than could be said about other parts of the house. In what passed for democracy in the nation, noble families beamed live images from their houses into the homes of their constituents, via their TV sets. It forced aristocrats to behave more stiffly than usual, artificially chivalrous and falsely courteous to staff. There was nothing real about their behaviour in front of the cameras. Only in their private bedrooms and bathrooms could they be themselves. You had to imagine what they got up to in there.

With thirty-four empty rooms spread around him, he pulled back the curtains to take a look at the sea in the distance. He reclined in the soft single bed, on a threshold of silence, and fell asleep.

An hour later he woke so dizzy with loneliness he had to fix his eyes upon the horizon to steady his spinning head. A full moon shimmered over the sea like tinfoil. Buoys winked their own personalised sequences. A pier was a sultry projection into the water. The sea breathed in the night like a lung.

Teirnon knocked and walked into the room, defying the usual protocol of waiting to be invited in. Pwyll sat up in his bed. He knew this was something extraordinary.

'I've come to tender my resignation,' Teirnon said.

The words passed through Pwyll like steel ghosts. He began hungering for air on that muggy, river-bottom of an evening. He mouthed, 'Why?' But Teirnon did not answer. 'Is it the money? I can improve your package.'

'No, my lord.'

'So tell me...'

'I'd rather not say.'

Pwyll began to speculate. 'Is this because we went to see your brother?'

'I'd rather not say.'

'Oh for God's sake...' Pwyll rose from the crumpled bed. 'I shot Arawn's dog, is that it?'

'I can make suggestions about my replacement.'

'I don't want a replacement,' he shouted, forcing Teirnon to look down at his boots. 'Take some time to think about it.'

'I don't need to think about it.'

'Then if you must...' Pwyll drew in his stomach to tighten the sound of his voice. 'I'll ask the accountant to arrange your back-end payments.'

Teirnon turned around and pulled the door shut behind him, leaving Pwyll listening to his own laboured breath.

By morning Teirnon had left the house. That was all the time he needed to pack up his possessions, to strike his presence from the estate he'd been associated with for thirty years. Pwyll sat on a Chesterfield in the lounge in front of a log fire that Teirnon had set – his last official duty before leaving. Pwyll watched it reduce to embers then ran out of the house.

Through the meadows he glided, beneath the hard cough of crows, the sodden grass licking at his ankles. When he reached his destination – a barn – he opened the rusting bolt and pulled back the double doors. From out of the gloaming his father's Bentley Azure grew in brightness like an energy-saving light bulb.

What a fucking motor. He sat in it and dreamed. He ran his fingers over the steering wheel. The smell of upholstery reminded him of his dad. A convertible with white kid-leather upholstery, lamb's-wool floor rugs, burr oak veneers, walnut steering wheel, digital radio, MP3 player, subwoofer and four channel amplifier, Sat Nav system, refrigerated bottle cooler... all this and the keys in the ignition.

There was eleven-year-old vintage high-octane fuel in the tank. Some had gone over the years exercising the car around the estate. More still had simply evaporated. There were about three gallons left, he reckoned. He could wait another eleven years to let that vanish into thin air, or take his father's advice and make the final journey count.

He turned the key. The battery was sluggish but the V8 engine came to life, making a sound no louder than a cat purring. He engaged the transmission. His father had been generous and solicitous. He rolled out of the barn, through the estate along the potholed tarmac. Hark! What's that sound? The rumble of wrought-iron gates rolling open on oiled castors. An invitation to hit the open road... how could he resist?

A mile from the house and already he'd smashed a wing mirror against a container dumped in the road. There were so many things to avoid, now that cars had had their day.

When he felt he'd got the hang of it he switched on the MP3 player. Violins and cymbals filled the car. His father's music had an emotional impact on him but may not have been the most appropriate comment on the souk he was fast approaching.

He followed a route marked out by Moroccan honeycomb lamps strung from stalls and tried not to kill anyone as he pushed the nose of the Bentley into the crowds. Boys looked down at him inside this great car and their hands came into the open cock-pit to touch his hair. He felt like a celebrity. But the car was the celebrity. They didn't love him. They loved the car. Being in a convertible he heard from outside several languages crunching like gears, transporting him he knew not where, and picked up all sorts of aromas – spices and wet dog.

He drew ever more people into the road and inhaled their spent breath. A few people recognised *him* passing through their ends. He had to drive over piles of broken porcelain and sheep carcases to get out of this souk, mounted the pavement once, corrected and then was out of the market for good.

At last he could put his foot down, climbing to 100 mph in ten seconds along the dual carriageway, past terraces of abandoned vehicles and their communities. Speed cameras, idle for a decade, were flashing behind him like the paparazzi. This was the A485 and once he veered off at exit seven he knew exactly where he wanted to go. He passed through housing estates where young girls walk to the playground and are never seen again, saw factories with not a single pane of glass intact. He floored the Bentley and his head kicked back into the leather headrest.

He'd been out an hour. The fuel gauge was

blinking on reserve. The music was full orchestra now, kettle drums and oily wood. He lurched around potholes and mounted grassy banks to avoid fallen trees and came within sight of a nexus of dwellings signalling Arawn's estate. He drove past farmhands tilling the soil, holding turnips in one hand, machetes in the other.

A white beach-pebble courtyard rang out the sound of tyres. The house itself was handsome gothic. Pwyll circled a lake that was stocked with rainbow trout snapping at flies stuck in the meniscus. The music ebbed and flowed through the subwoofer and of all things to suddenly remember, it was his father taking him to the dentist. That's where his dad had first heard this music, playing in the dentist's surgery. Pwyll had come to have a corrective procedure under general anaesthetic. As his dad asked the dentist about the music Pwyll felt a scratch on his arm and heard the anaesthesiologist ask where he'd like to go on holiday. He replied he'd like to go on safari in South Africa and then the next thing he knew he was sitting up in the recovery bed with a swollen clutter in his mouth, spittle gurgling, blood seeping down his throat.

He heard the last gasp of gasoline. He booted his foot to the boards and plunged the Bentley into the lake.

Fish bounced to the surface with the turbulence, their frigid eyes seeking out probable cause. Ice-cold water poured into the cockpit. The engine continued to run for a moment and then fizzled out. The MP3 player kept playing that same velvety music as he swam through the spectrum cast by the spill of oil.

Four men waiting at the edge of the lake he recognised from the hunting party. Now attired in military fatigues, they brought him roughly to his feet.

'Installation for your pond,' he said. 'So who's the daddy now?'

They escorted him into the library, where he stood dripping on the slate flagstones. Few people had libraries any more. He saw first editions from Laurence Sterne to W.G. Sebald. He heard the whirr of a camera picking up his presence. This one was for the DVD archives, a good show that would run and run. A servant came through oak doors to assist him out of his wet clothes and into dry ones.

Arawn came in and joined his men. He pointed to the seats around the table. As everyone sat down under a candle chandelier, he said to Pwyll, 'Thanks for the car, son. I'll have it dried and cured.'

'So, is this thing closed, with the dog?'

'Not quite. We've a problem with our neighbour, Havgan.'

'That's the second time I've heard that name.'

'Havgan's got airborne capability, flying rockets over the border. He's killed eight civilians in the past six months.'

'Rockets?'

'Fuelled... with what we don't know, burning under conventional warheads.'

Pwyll remained silent, wondering how this could be relevant to him.

'Your experience at the front might be useful to us.'

He saw, for the second time, a suppressed smile shimmer though the group of men. Then three Chinese maids brought in coffee and muffins on silver platters. Pwyll was given no time to enjoy the fare as Arawn had risen to his feet.

'Come with me please.'

They walked through the ringing house up the stairs and along the hall into Arawn's bedroom suite. Inside they startled his wife, who was sitting on the bed, reading an interiors magazine.

Arawn sat on the edge of the bed next to his wife and gathered up one of her arms, clutching it near his heart with those gravedigger's hands. 'Is it wrong to want to protect all I hold dear against this terrorist? This is Alma, my wife, by the way.'

Pwyll nodded slowly at her until she smiled back. 'Go undercover, find out how he's making rocket propellant. You'll work out of here.'

'I have my own cantrefs to protect,' Pwyll protested. 'I need to be seen there as you're seen here.'

'I'll protect your cantrefs, don't you worry. I have weeks and weeks of unseen CCTV footage I can run through to make it look like I'm still here.'

'You can do that?' Pwyll was still mindful of the woman on the bed.

'It does mean though that you'll have to sleep with my wife.'

What in the world did Pwyll have to go home for? It didn't feel much of a sacrifice to be Arawn for a while, and sleep with his beautiful wife. Within what seemed an indecently short time they were sitting at different ends of a long, wide Moroccan day bed talking like old friends. He hadn't really talked to a woman like this since his mother was alive, not a mature woman anyway. Alma was ten years older than Pwyll and ten years younger than her husband. Pwyll struggled to hide his feelings, but her scent kept stimulating him. The sight of fine downy hairs on her wrists as she moved her hands through the air made him light-headed.

She talked about many things, including her younger sister Rhiannon, who was too 'wild and petulant' for her own good, who rode better than any man, who refused to settle for less than the best and was more or less alone in the world as a consequence. 'It's all very well when you're young, to be idealistic, but not as you get older.' By this he assumed she was referring to her own age. He wanted to protest, but she began again. 'My sister's twenty-two, old enough to know better. Our father's planning to marry her off to the first bidder.'

He couldn't picture her sister. He was, however, intensely interested in Alma, who he could see all too clearly. 'Did you settle for less than the best?' he asked in all innocence.

She laughed briefly and a little bitterly, he thought. 'Did I settle for less? What would you say if I told you my husband prefers to spend all his time in the company of men?'

'I'd say he was blind.'

'There is another word for it.'

'If I was your husband I'd never leave your side.'

'Well now, you'll have that chance soon enough.'

Indeed he did. As she drew down the bed sheets, Alma said, 'Arawn only feels desire when he can act out a rape. Straightforward sex for him is as boring as eating. He wolfs down his food too, come to think of it.'

'I'd be gentle if I was in his shoes.'

'You are in his shoes.'

He daren't look at her, in case he saw there an invitation to seduce her, an invitation he'd find hard to refuse.

'I know you'd be gentle with me,' she continued, 'from just talking with you.'

'You do?' he was genuinely surprised.

'Sure. If you can talk to someone you can communicate in other ways too. Talking is the basis of everything.'

He did not sleep very much that night. He stayed on guard to watch her dozing lightly a few feet away on that commodious bed. It was hard not to imagine what he'd like to do to her, yet he remained paralysed, unable to act it out. He'd been taught never to violate another man's wife, a code passed down through the ages that he never questioned. He believed it was an endemically Welsh moral, when cowardice might have been its proper name.

The following morning he was first to wake – if he'd ever been to sleep. He allowed his fingers to touch the ends of her thick, black hair and her eyes sprung wide open. He bucked off the bed and turned his back in shame.

'It's okay,' she said. 'Come back here.'

'I daren't,' he answered, feeling her heat getting closer. 'I think I should contact Arawn and tell him I can't do this.'

'Havgan's not a noble, you know, he's an anarchist. I know how to find him for you.'

'You do?' he said turning, so easily bribed.

'His daughter worked in our kitchens last summer. She has little love for her father.'

The way she was looking at him made his voice shake. 'Arawn must know her too, then?'

'Arawn knows nothing. He hasn't been into our kitchens for decades. I told you, if you can talk you can communicate about many things.' She smiled. 'You've been respectful to me, and I'm grateful, even though my husband doesn't deserve such an honourable friend.'

Pwyll met with Havgan's daughter in a coffee shop in town. An undistinguishable and rather morbid girl in her late teens, with black painted fingernails and black eyeliner under her eyes, she made him work for the intelligence on her father.

'What's in it for me?' was her opening remark.

Anticipating this, he slid an envelope across the table. She picked it up and looked inside.

Her eyes widened within the black whorl. 'What do you want to know?'

'I need to find out where he makes fuel.'

'I can tell you where his place of business is. Stinks to high heaven.'

'What business?'

'He's the dog-food king, I'm embarrassed to say.'

He looked around the café. There were quite a few teenagers inside, drinking darkly from coffee cups and smoking. None of them paid much attention to Pwyll. He wasn't recognised outside his own cantrefs. Such a relief, not to have to be ready with the appropriate royal response; it felt like he was on a moral holiday.

She told him where her father could be found. And then she told him how he should be approached.

'You say... my mother is beside herself with pain. I want to help her die.'

His mother was already dead, but still he asked, 'I really say that?'

'It's what I hear other people say. Always something that ends with, I want to help her die, and then he takes them inside his factory.'

Pwyll had not taken many steps in life that weren't ordained for him by others. He couldn't think of a single major act he'd managed on his own volition. And here he was again, acting on orders that seemed to have befallen him.

Mounted up and heading along the old motorway, with a hand-drawn map in his hands, he practised the lines he was to use on Havgan. He turned off at exit fifteen and was soon catching the highlights of kids ripping copper pipes off the wall of a house. A car burned at the side of the road, with people walking casually by as if this were nothing special. From shop to light manufacturing unit, there was precious little glass left anywhere in one piece.

He found the factory surrounded by a three-metre-high wall, crowned with broken glass. Inside were six storage silos. A drying tower puffed out emissions that smelled of burning flesh, and worse. He progressed through the iron gates into the compound. As he dismounted within a circle of caravans, cars, vans and pick-ups, Dobermans and pit bulls came off the ground at speed, drooling and snarling, straining at their chains pegged to the ground. His horse's eyes bulged like ducks' eggs.

A man broke cover from inside a caravan and quieted the alarm system with a tossed leg of rotting mutton. He looked at Pwyll in a questioning fashion.

Pwyll said, 'I'm looking to help my mother die.'

'It'll be Havgan you want then,' he replied and beckoned to an arena fenced in by galvanised-iron sheets, pallets and old tyres. At the far end was a portakabin with steel bars across the windows.

He walked through a bunch of chickens scratching around in the mud and entered the door of the portakabin. A rather brutal-looking man with shaved bullet-head, dressed in blue overalls, was sitting behind a desk. He stared at Pwyll with the same silent aggression as the guy in charge of the dogs.

Pwyll tried out his rehearsed request. It was all he had to defend himself. 'My mother's beside herself with pain and I want to help her die.'

'My daughter sent you, did she?'

He didn't expect that response. 'Yes,' he said, not knowing what else to say.

'So you'll have seen she's a dreamer. It's always books with her. Gets nothing if it doesn't exist in a book.'

Pwyll could hear workers swearing outside in the yard. Havgan leaned across to the window and closed the Venetian blinds.

'My place of business appalls my daughter so much she won't come here. I tell her, this business paid for your education... ah, don't let me get started!'

But it had started and Pwyll could see a theme take shape. Havgan clutched his chest and looked up, speaking into the broken bulb in the ceiling as though it hid a microphone recording his words for prosperity.

'My daughter reads too many books that aren't like life. She looks for happiness where there is none.' He spilled a cracked, yellow laugh. 'But perhaps you can only understand these things when looking back at them. Not something you can see in advance.'

He stopped when a woman came into the portakabin and started sweeping the floor. He splayed his hands on the desk and cleaned his fingernails with a spent match picked out of an ashtray. He lifted up his feet to allow her to sweep under the desk. She wore a wrap printed with yellow flowers and a matching cloth coiled around her head. Her skin was a dark inky blue.

Havgan let his shoes clatter back to the floor. He stood up so fast the cleaner flinched. 'So you want to euthanise your granddad, do you?'

'My mother,' Pwyll corrected.

'Not many people have the balls.'

Pwyll followed him out of the portakabin, waded through the hens, edged round the dogs straining in their collars then rammed through several sets of Perspex doors to reach the heart of the factory.

The view before him took many seconds to comprehend. On the concrete floor was a mountain of 4-D livestock – the dead, dying, diseased and disabled. He could see one old heifer still trembling, breathing steam through dilated nostrils. Sticking out of the pile were hooves, heads, road kill, supermarket meats still packaged. There were euthanised dogs and cats still wearing flea collars. Oozing down the sides was offal, intestines, udders, spleen, chicken backs and frames. A hundred thousand maggots writhed and sizzled.

Three men in balaclava masks loaded all this into a machine. Plus cement-kiln dust, newsprint, cattle and pig manure. The machine was like a giant, top-loader washing machine, with steam under high pressure leaking from its joints. Squeezed out the other end was a long sausage-like tube of what he assumed was either dog food or highly combustible rocket fuel.

'Smell something awful, don't it?' Havgan said. 'But how would farmers live without me? That's forty per cent of their product. Anything not fit for human consumption ends up in my extruder.'

He keyed open a storeroom and turned on some battery illumination. Inside were sacks of grains, flour and large tins of chemicals. He unlocked a padlock on an aluminium chest. When Havgan beckoned him to take a look inside the trunk Pwyll saw a selection of small arms. A Russian Baikal gas pistol, some kind of low-powered blank firer drilled through, a Makarov 9mm and a converted blowback operated double-action 1ZH shotgun.

From this chest Havgan removed a half-litre bottle marked with the words 'Fatal Plus'. He wrapped it in an old sheet splattered with primrose-yellow paint and stuffed it into a blue rucksack that was hanging from a hook.

'Administer that to your grandfather,' Havgan said.

'*Mother*,' Pwyll said.

'To her, give five grams of this shit and it's good-night Irene.'

What the bottle contained exactly, he went to some trouble to explain. 'It's what vets use to put animals down. Puts them in a coma, induces respiratory apnea and in thirty minutes they're dead. As for what it is exactly, it's a schedule two barbiturate. You can IV it or take it orally. But orally it needs a little sweetener added.

'Some people like to check-out early,' he continued. 'That's why I got some – from the vets, to sell to euthanasia groups, who deserve more support than they get. My dear old dad died in extreme pain so now I like to contribute something to others suffering from incurable cancers, etc, who just want to die. It's definitely not a profit-making venture, but a service to people who'd otherwise have to travel to Mexico to buy the stuff, since it's banned everywhere else. Clinical name's sodium pentobarbital, the same basic stuff as the Nembutal that saw off Marilyn Monroe.' He then gave Pwyll a searching look. 'What's your grandmother's name?'

'My mother, it's for my mother...'

'I know, your mother. Just checking you weren't trying to pull one over on me.' He thrust the rucksack into Pwyll's hands. 'Give her a swig of that and say cheers from me.'

As soon as he was able he met with Arawn's men to pass on the intelligence. They sat in the library and using ordnance survey maps and late-twentieth-century photo plots, pinpointed exactly where the plant was.

Within a few more hours he prepared to leave the house, and head back to his own country seat. Among his clothes in the suitcase he hid the small bottle of Fatal Plus given to him by Havgan. He didn't want to leave it behind in case someone ingested it by mistake.

Alma interrupted him while he was packing. She came into the bedroom crying. 'Won't you lie with me one last time before you go?' She began to peel off her clothes.

'No, no...' he said.

'Yes,' she insisted and held his hand against her naked breast. 'Now, can you resist?'

He retrieved his hand, wrapped his arms around his chest and closed his eyes.

'You can't stop me dreaming,' she said.

He said, 'I'm dreaming too,' and relented, lying

53

back with her against silk cushions, watching the pale moon through branches of trees sway like water in a jar.

'I'll miss you,' she said. 'Arawn's a lot to live up to.'

A warm breeze entered the room from the wide-open French windows. About three kilometres away smoke began to rise from what Pwyll now understood to be Havgan's fuel-producing plant. His quiet time with Alma was ruptured suddenly by a loud bang from the plant. Seconds later came a dull muted thump, and then the tearing of bellows, a hiss of leaking gas. They both sat up and saw a flash of light, like a creamy torch light up the sky. An aerial vapour cloud blossomed and touched down between the darkened buildings. The lower level envelope slumped towards the fields outside the plant and made a footprint there. With a second, much louder bang, scaffolding legs flew upwards, spiralling back like sycamore pods.

All this in the first eighteen seconds. Then the vapour cloud detonated. They felt its hot wind in their faces, heard a roaring in their ears. The noise of the fire made a rasping, sucking noise – like a child drinking to the bottom of a milkshake through a straw.

On the bed with Arawn's semi-naked wife, Pwyll was soon wondering what it would be like to sail away from all that hissing, jangling fire. So cool a thought, he had to wonder where it came from and where he actually was. But in his heart he knew that the moment was unique, the end of one thing and the beginning of another. He focused all his attention on that image of a yacht carrying him out to the sea on wind and tidal power alone. What a fine thing, to travel in silence to where the air is crystal-clean, pure and moist.

That would be a good end. It was the end of something.

Two

After his adventures in Alma's bedroom, Pwyll pined for her intimacies, *somebody's* intimacies. He needed to find a woman of his own before he turned into a sorry person. His parents would have been making arrangements for him right now. But they were dead and so this was something he was going to have to fix for himself.

He took to riding into villages, looking into young women's faces from his saddle. But none of them appealed. No one looked anything like Alma and he couldn't bring himself to step down from the horse to investigate further. What he did notice though, was the way his people appeared on the road to call out his name. They smiled instead of doffing their hats. Something had made them more appreciative.

Same thing in town: early morning the binge emporiums and grog factories had their doors flung open, airing out the stench of beer and cigarettes. Revellers, drunks, teenagers and DJs stumbling out into the light and when they saw him, called out his name in spontaneous, ribald fashion.

His new steward, at the stables to meet him, was about ten years younger than Teirnon but just as obsequious. 'Greetings my lord, what a fine morning you've had for a ride.'

'Actually I've had the warmest reception while out riding. What's going on? Something got into the water supply?'

'Arawn's got into them, my lord.' The steward unbuckled the saddle from beneath the horse's belly. 'While you were away, he ordered a public flogging of five gangsters in the square... in your name, mind you.'

'That's what they want from me is it, a firmer hand?'

'Violence in the cantrefs is four-hundred times higher than in 1950, Arawn said. Though, fair dos, only European example of a crime-free community is Lapland.'

'Is that so?' Pwyll was beginning to feel a little miffed. 'What do they do up there to keep the peace, I wonder?'

The steward continued to stable the horse while singing Arawn's praises. 'He's done some very tidy things round here on your behalf, he has.'

'Oh do tell.'

'Like, pass legislation protecting healthcare for the unemployed.'

'What!'

'Hell of a boy, Arawn.'

Pwyll began to feel envious of Arawn's seemingly effortless ability to make popular decisions. He took some compensatory pleasure in recalling Alma, and how she'd enjoyed his company more than her husband's. But unlike Arawn's public achievements this private one was not for bragging over.

The next time he rode out looking for a wife he decided to travel further afield. He took the horse through suburban zones until they gave way to thickening countryside, to clusters of willows draped over dry stone walls, where lines of poplars stood out against pure white skies. The folly of this decision only struck him then: there were no women to view, just wild horses spooking his steed.

He went as far west as the land would allow and arrived at the sea. He let the horse amble along the coastal path and stared out at the gently rollicking sea until he couldn't think straight any more.

So what now? What was a lord meant to do with too much time on his hands? No women, no work, just time-wasting activities such as hunting. He'd even lost his interest in that. Ahead he could see the low-lying peninsula bending around and jutting into the sea. Shimmering in the sun it didn't look a solid form. Around him the air was acoustically dead. The cadence of the sea began to infiltrate his random thoughts until each blended perfectly with the other. A razorbill glided sluggishly over the water. A strong wind followed behind, tugging at the sun-burnt grass around the horse's hooves and shattering his reverie.

He became morose then, looking over the edge of the footpath at the hundred-metre drop below and at the small container ship beached on the rocks, leaning over on the keel. The sight of her like that seemed indecent somehow, with her body rusting, all port windows smashed, intestines spilled onto the rocks.

Something else, some*one* caught his eye. A woman was leading her horse down on the shore, her orange cotton shift like fire burning oxygen out of the air. Even from that distance he could detect in her face that she was watching him, assessing his significance; how the fearful watch the unknown.

She disoriented him, made him doubt his bearings. But when he lost sight of her behind a cliff face he plunged into a state of instant mourning. Here was something he must act upon, no question. He yanked his horse off the path and up the hill into a meadow of scarlet bells and orange daisies. From this greater height he got sight of her again and with it came instant relief. She was side on, her hair hiding her face.

Then she disappeared once more, although an

after-image of her Indian cotton shift remained.

This was beginning to look like a tease, or a subtle but deliberate move on her behalf to avoid an encounter with a stranger. He was determined to find out either way and gave the horse a kick. He descended the path to come closer to shore, got a full view of the bay each way, and she was gone.

The next few moments were unbearable ones. He even wondered if he'd been hallucinating, if this woman was born from his own starvation. Then beyond a copse of cultivated trees he saw a cottage – small, rustic, whitewashed, its door ajar. A horse was tethered up outside. His heart began beating so fast it made his ribs ache.

In one continuous move he dismounted, spun the reins around a brass hoop attached to the cottage wall and stepped across the threshold, lowering his head to clear the doorframe. The kitchen was busy with earthenware pots stuffed with cut flowers. Shelves were stacked with herbs, cans of powdered milk, dried beans. Carrots, beetroots and potatoes filled a wicker basket sitting on the flagstone floor. The scrubbed wooden table, buckled and grooved, supported more flowers in vases.

The heavy scent of bridal-white flowers acted like a narcotic upon him, numbing him to someone's entrance from another room. A woman stood in the kitchen for several seconds without speaking, maintaining a physical distance while assessing the situation, and looking very severe. Her skin was folded from exposure to the sun, the strong eyes surrounded by faint crow's feet. Her raven hair had acquired its first grey streaks.

'The door was open,' he explained.

'And you took that as an invitation?'

'I had to know who you were.'

'I know who you are.'

'I am Lord...'

'Alma told me about you.'

'Alma?' He lit up with the sound of her name. 'You know Alma?'

'She's my sister. Come... let's take a walk outside. I don't trust you well enough just yet to invite you into my home.'

He followed her outside and began strolling towards the lighthouse. 'What did Alma tell you about me?' he asked.

She held up a hand, pushing it towards his face to silence him. He felt a little angry at her for trying to prevent him speaking.

'In time all will be revealed.'

'Do you live in that cottage?'

'When I am in need of peace and solitude, I do.'

'How often is that?'

She shook her head empathically. 'When I want to talk I'll let you know.'

This was more than he could cope with. He was coming apart at the seams. It was a mistake, pursuing this woman out here. Alma had spoken of her sister as insatiable and idealistic. But she also seemed disturbed in some way, and unstable women frightened him. His mother had been unstable, overpowering him with her love or withdrawing it on a whim.

She led the way in silence until they reached the lighthouse, where hundreds of birds lay dead at their feet. Every night, she explained, birds fluttered around the lighthouse, creating a blizzard effect in the rotating beams. The ones lying dead on the ground had flown too eagerly at the light.

She was willing to talk about the dead, but not the living.

He tried to imagine her existence on this salt-blasted peninsula. He wondered if she slept alone. He couldn't tell anything by looking at her, so kept one eye on the clouds forming over the sea and the other on the coastal path along which they progressed in single file. At a chambered entrance under a granite slab she turned around to him. 'They found a medieval skeleton inside there, sitting up and begging. A female recluse who'd come here to die. This whole area was once inhabited by women.'

As it is again, he thought.

She told him, 'King Arthur's buried here too.'

He smiled to himself.

'Maybe Arthur came for the women.'

'I imagined you'd say that.'

'Did you?' He was surprised. Her guess seemed to be more a gift of clairvoyance than knowledge. It seemed that in order to understand her he was just going to have to read the sky and sea and the stones in this Zen garden of hers.

He decided she must have come here to die, along with the other female recluses who hoped to find peace in a mild climate. Certainly there was a feel of death this far west, emanating from the rocks that pierced the sea. They too were burial grounds, but for sailors who'd not chosen to die. For slaves who'd not even chosen to sail. Those rocks, like rows of broken teeth, were an image for the end of all journeys.

She caught up with him, and was saying, 'Out here I understand the futility of living in the future. Birds and fish don't live in the future, why should we.'

If that remark was bland and stupid, it also human-ised her, made her seem less untouchable. 'Birds and fish think about what's for dinner ahead of time,' he said as warmly as possible. 'That's living in the future.'

She released a tiny laugh from the back of her throat. Then without him seeing it, she slipped her hand inside his arm. He hardly dared move off the spot.

'Can we talk now, about living things?' he asked.

'I said I would tell you when.' She took back her arm and sprinted off along the path that led back to the cottage.

In her little garden they sat at a wicker table as the daylight receded over the land. They drank tea with powdered milk, ate freshly baked soda bread with peanut butter. He was relaxed enough to take long glances at her.

Then she said, 'I brought you out here so I could take a look at you.'

'You brought *me* out here?'

She became sombre all of a sudden. 'I'm being set up to marry a man I despise.'

Instantly he felt flocked around by the world and the air grew darker.

Alma had said: our father's going to marry her off to the first man who comes along.

'Don't you have the option to refuse?' he asked.

'You know how it is: parents offer their daughters to consolidate their power.' She paused for a moment.

'Alma said you were the man I should be marrying.'

66

He was a little startled by her directness. 'But you don't know me.'

'I know more about you than the man I am to marry.' Her accent had a ringing tone he couldn't place. 'Do you find me attractive?'

He did, she was, but he answered: 'I don't know yet.'

'That's cute! You have to know someone before you can tell if they're attractive?'

Feeling himself redden he turned his face away towards her elaborate garden, the star-shaped yellow flowers draped over the perimeter wall. Edging the lawn he recognised Hottentot fig, a South African ice plant with magenta flowers that could survive gales and driving salt spray. In the beds were clusters of Red Campion, pink Oxalis from South America, Mediterranean Bear's Breeches, Arum lilies and Whistling Jacks. He heard Rhiannon say something else about Alma, but missed it.

'When did you acquire this cottage?'

'It was my mother's and her mother's before that. They planted everything, made it nice. Women need a place to run to. Their marriages were arranged as well.'

As darkness began to fall, shearwaters returning from feeding binges in the Atlantic made a shrieking noise from the coast. He felt he was in the wrong place, inside the wrong skin.

Against all instinct, he made moves to take his leave. She did not try to delay him, but as they walked to the horses she asked if he needed to stay the night. He declined immediately. Why was this? He didn't really know, but as a virgin he could not seem to make the leap from talking to her to sleeping in the same house as her in one move.

But he did ask if he could see her again.

She replied and this time her voice sounded like ripping fabric. 'Next time we meet I'll be married to this man Gwawl.'

'Just say no to him.'

'No one says no to Gwawl and lives to tell the tale.'

From the saddle he looked intently at her, waited for what more there was to come. He had to subdue his mutinous horse that was eager to get going.

She produced a felt pen from a pocket in her skirt and wrote down a date on his calf-leather saddle. 'That's my engagement party, at my uncle Heveydd's court. I'll put you on the guest list.'

'Why should I come to your engagement party?'

'To ravish me,' she said, without humour.

'What do you mean?'

'Do you want me to spell it out for you? We go to a room together. Shag. I arrange for us to get caught by one of Gwawl's people. He's only interested in marrying a virgin.'

He was all for trying to upset an archaic practice but this seemed a flimsy way of going about it. In any case he said he'd be there, before taking his leave and easing the horse along the footpath, across vertiginous overhangs. Not once did he look behind him. There was nothing but air below. That gap, that strip of nothing between him and the sea he decided was a metaphor for love at first sight. It could end up leading to his death.

If his life had been too easy to date, now it was not easy enough. Everyone was pushing him around. He felt less of a man than ever. Perhaps he could ask to go back into the army, join his regiment for a spot of search and destroy. All he could manage as a way of asserting himself was shooting rabbits on the lawn from his bedroom window. But the moment he saw an animal fall, his bottom lip began to quiver with regret.

The days leading up to Rhiannon's engagement party he spent on the sofa looking at the family photograph albums and eating caramelised popcorn. When the moment came to saddle up he spun out of the stables, stir crazy as all hell, mad at his parents for abandoning him, for not giving him siblings for company, and raced into Heveydd's cantref with pornography on his mind.

On Heveydd's land farm labourers stopped to watch him pass, standing still as scarecrows in the shadow of the Norman church spire. At the grand court he gave his horse to be stabled and in the mansion house was shown to a large bathroom where he could change into his dinner jacket. In black tie he progressed to the banquet hall. He heard the crowd before he saw it, a distant thunder of laughter rolling down the corridor.

Around a hundred people had congregated at the tables, raising pre-dinner cocktails and champagne flutes under spluttering candle chandeliers. Rhiannon found him almost as soon as he entered. She was ravishing in a sequin-covered bodice. She squeezed his arm and he tried not to stare at her cleavage.

'Which one is Gwawl?' he asked.

'Easy cowboy, he's not here yet.'

He was introduced to Heveydd, who distractedly shook Pwyll by the hand, looking over his shoulder at who else he might have preferred to talk to. Rhiannon had supervised the seating plan and sat Pwyll between herself and Heveydd.

The empty chair next to Rhiannon was reserved for Gwawl.

'What am I meant to do?' Pwyll asked. 'When he gets here?'

'Kiss me on the mouth. Then we go off to a bedroom.'

'Do you really think that's going to work?'

'When we get discovered, it will.'

The waiters arrived bringing soup tureens to the table and pouring wine into goblets. The soup was leek and potato with a hint of paprika. Huge platters of suckling pig were placed on the table along with live trout pools. The trout were brought out of the water and fillets sliced off their backs as they writhed on the platter. The heads continued to twitch as the fillets were seared on hot bricks from the ovens.

He followed a Chardonnay with a Bordeaux.

Gwawl had still not appeared and he was getting drunker.

Everyone was laughing, drinking. Rhiannon departed from the table to use the ladies' room and in her absence he saw, edging into the room, a man wearing sunglasses – a strange affectation. But he moved so slowly, and from the glistening in his eyes seen from the side, Pwyll assumed he was blind. In black tie also, his rich wavy hair was grey but still anchored low on the forehead and sticking up at the side as though he'd just now been yanked out of bed. Pwyll saw creases in his neck as deep as knife wounds. Something about this figure moved him so when he stopped beside Pwyll, he grew rather expectant.

He felt a hand introduce itself under his arm and then he and the blind man took each other off like a courting couple. He did not challenge this action, in thrall to this older blind man, but his limbs were numb from sitting and his head swimming with alcohol. They went into the kitchen which smelled of ammonia. Whoever did the cleaning was old school. The man removed his dark glasses and rubbed his soulful, mahogany eyes.

'Most of my life I've eaten fat-free, salt-free, exercised, never smoked, drank sparingly, got to old age and then lost my fucking sight. They never warn you about that, do they? Now I'm putting on the weight I've kept off all my life.'

Pwyll was mesmerised by those ruined, crashed eyes. Even blind, there was something fierce and magical about his presence, a heady mix of the lyrical and the bold. The romantic disposition of this man was beginning to overwhelm him.

'I need a favour granted,' the man asked.

'Yours to ask and mine to give.'

'Whatever I ask?'

Pwyll tried to think straight but the wine was working against caution. 'As long as it lies within my power.'

'It will, I assure you.'

'Then ask me what you will and you shall have it.'

'Let us first go back to the party.'

Again, Pwyll did not question this and submitted to being guided back to the table. Rhiannon had still not yet returned.

The blind man tapped a fork against a crystal goblet until the whole room was hushed. Pwyll laughed nervously. He noticed he was the youngest in the room by some margin.

Rhiannon came back into the hall and Pwyll caught sight of her contortion as she observed these new developments. The blind man grinned... at her, Pwyll thought.

Into the silence he spoke in a voice that brought

to mind Richard Burton in that old film, *The Assas-sination of Trotsky* that he'd once watched as a child on Sky's Film classics:

'Lord Pwyll, whatever favour I ask you will grant?'

'Your wish shall be my command.' He reverted to cliché.

'Don't promise anything!' Rhiannon shouted across the table.

'The favour I ask is that you step away from my fiancée.'

Pwyll's mouth fell open as his facial muscles atro-phied. He stood slowly up from the table, gripping the edge of the damask. He and Rhiannon brushed shoulders as he was trying to get out of the hall. She was scared and trembling. 'I hadn't marked you down as dumb,' she whispered in his ear. 'Let a pair of sunglasses fool you...'

'It was a stupid idea in the first place, my coming here. How did he know *why* I was here? You must have told someone.'

'No... yes. Oh, God!'

They both heard that clink of steel on crystal glass

again. Through the second silence he'd summoned, Gwawl roared: 'Why not make this engagement banquet our wedding feast!'

Two big men entered the hall, brushing aggressively against Pwyll and stationed themselves behind Gwawl. They did not look like they had come for dinner, carrying 7.62mm rifles and 9mm pistols. Gwawl was waiting for a reply from Rhiannon.

She bowed and said with mock graciousness, 'I ask you, my lord for a few weeks to prepare myself.'

'Granted.' Gwawl sat down heavily. 'Then we'll have a banquet to make this look like a dog's dinner.'

Outside the hall Pwyll locked himself into a bathroom with Rhiannon. 'I will never give myself to him!' she sobbed. 'I'll kill myself first.'

'Don't say that, Rhiannon.'

'I will kill myself. Or kill him.'

'There must be a way. One's life is not for others to determine.' Pwyll thought about what he'd just said. It was only true for men.

He fled the house, pushing his horse to the point of death over the wet sands of a three-mile beach.

Hardly was he home when an idea came to him. A desperate, last-ditch and dirty idea, but the only one he had. He put in a request with Gwawl's office for an informal, face-to-face. Given the circumstances of their one and only meeting, permission was granted.

Gwawl chose Starbucks as the venue in which to discuss what gifts he'd like Pwyll to bestow on him and his new bride.

By the end of that day, someone would be dead.

The same horse under him, Pwyll galloped across the same three-mile beach in the opposite direction. Nothing moved but that chestnut mare. In the light of early evening the wide expanse of wet sand was a marble floor, given extra depth by embedded muscovite, quartz, chalk and limestone, speckled with weed and streaked with coal. Clouds were threatening a downpour.

He wound his way into town along Walter Road and the steep incline of Princess Way where his horse became too anguished to ride over the slippery cobblestones. The feral dogs and the feral children also made her nervous, so Pwyll parked and blinkered her in a quiet stable before continuing on foot.

It had been a decade since he'd stepped into this southern city, but never had he remembered it as a shanty town. Half of all the shops were boarded up behind chipboard. Those still open for business were trading under incongruous names: Coggers, Boosh, Sapore. Four large chapels had been converted into a mega-restaurant, good-time casino, second-tier factory and big box store. Bouncers stood priestly outside gaping glass doors.

An entire Regency street half a mile long had been given over to nightclubs with names like Top Notch, Quids Inn, Zanzi Bar. It was a little after six in the evening and already cleaners were hosing vomit off the pavements outside. Squeezed between the clubs were a Baguette Du Jour, a defunct mobile phone boutique – Madam *Foner* – and a window of knickers on display at La Senza. 'Cappuccino... latte' was the writing on the wall. Even McDonald's was pushing the stuff. Firemen collected money in buckets and nurses cash in bedpans. Armed police patrolled in a horse-drawn van.

He had to hand it to them: the boys in the town planning department had really fucked up here. He even thought he recognised a few of them – parading about with hands in trouser pockets, surveying the place like generals, bulging out of pinstripe suits, their faces claret red. Only men who knew precisely nothing could create this bedlam. He'd heard somewhere that the brewery directors who owned the drinking clubs were these same town planners, who cried out for sanctions against young drunks.

Several young boys streaked past on bikes and skateboards. He caught up with them at a brick-and-steel water feature down the end of the crashed thoroughfare. He tried listening to their raised, hysterical voices but couldn't understand a word. A new language was forming in the land. Three generations of pregnant women, all from the same family by the look of them, were smoking heavily, guarding the water feature like the Sphinx. He saw Africans and Asians where once there'd been none. Elegant, composed and sober, they appeared in a state of shock in their new land, in the presence of the indigenous tribe.

It was Saturday and the air rancid with fried fat. Tinkling sounds of highlife guitar rose and fell on clouds of steam. He came upon a thicket of trellis tables with displays of coconuts, sheep heads, wood carvings, cones of multi-coloured spices. He was tempted with dyed fabrics and shown displays of cheap jewellery while feeling a hand frisk his back pocket. Two boys ran away, but with nothing to show for it. He handled scarves, handbags, pottery. He looked at sunglasses, shampoos.

When the rain came down he ducked into a WH Smith then Boots the Chemist, and finally gave into fatigue at a camping goods store. He crawled inside a two-man tent erected on the shop floor and laid back, feet sticking out of the flap. He'd not slept all last night from worrying about the day's meeting. The rain outside came down with a long whistling howl. He closed his eyes and the rain took on a deeper significance.

On summer days in adolescence, he used to stroll

on a hot beach with his boarding-school friends. He loved those friends for keeping his rank a secret when out and about among the civilians. He was just one of the lads pounding the coastal path, with the hot sun in his salty hair, the colour of the blue sea in his eyes, the green ferns scratching his naked arms. At Tears Point on Langland, the sea expanded ocean-wise. It was wild and windy and a little dangerous and he could never quite control his thoughts out there. Other days they'd walk in the opposite direction to Rothers Sker where houses with green and ochre tiles facing the sea helped root him to the place. The imagination was not engaged at Rothers Sker, but the heart was. They'd jump into the sea from off the rocks and swim back to the beach, then walk past families playing cricket on hard sand, the clapboard changing huts, the Surfside Café and the St Johns First Aid hut where he'd once had a stitch sewn into his lip. All the while with the warmth of the sun on his skin. He tried not to look at the girls lying on towels in bikinis, drinking coke and smoking. He wanted to engage with them but his courage always failed him.

He waited until winter to do that, at the one o'clock club at the Top Rank. He waded out onto the dance floor and touched one of these girls on the shoulder, as was the protocol. If she wished to dance she would, or turn her back if not. She danced with him, each painfully saying nothing. An old or maybe current boyfriend came over from a dark corner and challenged him to a fight. The girl smiled at her friends. She got her kicks from such encounters. The only way he could get out of it was by calling in the Secret Service, or going through the toilet windows.

He took the latter option and baled out into the Kingsway. From there he ran into Castle Street and hid inside a basement snooker club where boozers languished between afternoon closing and evening opening. When his friends caught up with him they played a few frames then emerged into the failing light to the sound of barkers selling the *Evening Post* outside the market, and the evangelists patrolling the cinema queue, warning young couples that the devil lay waiting for them inside. Gradually gamblers, snooker players, sailors and soldiers, those *Evening Post* barkers began converging on the pubs. For kids like Pwyll the issue was how to get a drink under age. The cocktail bar in the Dolphin Hotel usually obliged as a last resort – also a venue for gays. On this occasion, the All Blacks rugby team was resident in the hotel and Pwyll sunk three pints under their quizzical gaze. A giant from Dunedin offered to fuck him, so they escaped into the cold air again. Drunk and happy they glided towards the Macabre Café, where bikers were lacing their coca-colas with aspirin... then a shop assistant was tugging at his foot, telling him the camping store was closing...

Groggy and ripe, he set off at a pace through the raining and swinging streets, past ruins and boys in their ruin, fearful of the time he'd lost. He had wanted to get to the meeting before Gwawl.

But Gwawl had beaten him to it, lounging in a window seat. His two bodyguards were there too, and looked sprung from cages. They patted Pwyll down before inviting him to sit. Starbucks was moderately full, the place lit by whale-oil lamps. Coffee was roasted and water boiled over woodchip fires in a modified pizza oven.

This was Gwawl's venue of choice. As Pwyll pulled up a chair he said, 'You like Starbucks? I like Starbucks. Never see a fight in Starbucks. Only civilised place in town.'

They had yet to order and the bare table in front of them came as some relief to Pwyll. 'Can I get you gentlemen something to drink?'

'The big spender!' Gwawl said and they all laughed. The bodyguards ordered mocha milkshakes. Gwawl asked for a caramel frappuccino with whipped cream.

'Tall or grande?' Pwyll asked.

'Grande, if you're buying.'

'In or out?' the girl serving asked Pwyll.

'In,' he said and added an espresso to the order.

He paid the bill and waited for the drinks. The mocha milkshakes arrived first, followed by the espresso and then the caramel frappuccino. Pwyll glanced over at the table. He popped the cap on the vial inside his pocket. He took another fast look around. His nerve ends were singing with dread. He poured 10ml of sodium pentobarbital into each of the three drinks. He dumped the vial into the bin and stirred the drinks with a little wooden stick, careful not to dislodge the head of whipped cream on the frappuccino. The door of the café opened and he felt a cool breeze rolling in off the sea.

'You want a tray for those?' the serving girl asked.

He loaded the drinks onto the tray and headed off for the table. It felt a long walk on weak legs. His knees were knocking together. He concentrated intensely on the load.

He arrived in time to hear Gwawl ask one of his bodyguards, 'So how did you do it, blow up BP?'

The window looked out into the road, empty for now, where the rain was falling silently. He carefully removed the drinks from the tray, making sure they went to the right people.

'How did I do it? *Why* did I do it!' the bodyguard said, absentmindedly taking his drink from the table and slurping from the rim. 'Because I was arrogant.

Arrogance makes you stupid.'

'This is not caramel frappuccino is it?' Gwawl asked, inhaling the aroma.

'Yes it is.'

'Doesn't smell like it.'

'It's definitely caramel frappuccino.'

'Smells like the milk's gone off,' said one of the bodyguards.

'Looks like hot chocolate,' said the other.

'What did BP do to you to make you so mad, then?'

'There was no end of things I felt indignant about, things going wrong in the world,' the bodyguard continued.

'Like what?' Gwawl asked. 'What did you feel indignant about?' He stuck his tongue into the whipped cream. 'Why did you get hot chocolate when I asked for caramel frap, Pwyll?'

'If someone orders you to do something,' the bodyguard continued, 'you should always consider doing the exact opposite, is what I've learnt.'

Something in Pwyll's head stretched so taut his

vision became blurred. His eyes were barely open when he heard himself say, 'For fuck's sake, it's what you ordered, Gwawl.'

The table became a still life around him.

'Excuse me?' the bodyguard said.

The other bodyguard said, 'I'll drink it if you don't want it!'

Pwyll's hand was on his wrist. 'I bought it for him, not you.'

'Now, now, boys,' said Gwawl, calming things between his bodyguards and Pwyll. He grabbed the paper cup from off the table and swallowed hard and long.

The ceiling pressed down upon Pwyll's head. Now, more than ever, he hoped he'd killed one of those Moroccan insurgents at the front. Families sprouted everywhere, baby buggies blocked the aisles. Voices around him became like an echo beneath the sea. 'She tells you to do something and if you don't do it you get told off...'

'I know what I want for my wedding present,' Gwawl opened up the discussion. 'A stud-horse. Arab stallion. That'll do for me. For Rhiannon, I, uh, oh, a bottle of sherry should suffice.'

The father of a small boy at the next table said, 'That's boys for you!' He was in his twenties, prematurely balding and speaking to his wife. 'This Daniel in his class...'

Pwyll was thinking hard and it wasn't going anywhere. There was no exhaust. He looked outside at the late blooming flowers in window boxes, the deep green of trees lining the street, the darkening sky.

The little boy on the next table said, 'He hasn't been to sleep for nine years.'

Pentobarbital induces respiratory apnea and in thirty minutes you're dead.

'Who hasn't been to sleep?'

'My cat.'

Then it changed, the atmosphere in Starbucks. Kids began crying, falling down and hitting their heads on table legs, jamming fingers in toilet doors. The girl serving was raising her voice to four teenagers at the counter. Did they want something or not? She would not ask again. Her voice was edged with childish impatience. This was the last time she would ask. This was their final call.

'I'll get you the horse,' Pwyll said and stood.

'Where you going? You've only just got here.'

'Things to do, you know how it is.'

He turned and walked out of Starbucks as slowly as he could manage on burning feet, into the driving rain. Immediately he became welded to events developing around him in a street laced with bottomless sobs. There must have been a few hundred people out and about and none were sober, none over fourteen. There was a long line outside the fish and chip shop that traded in Class A drugs to keep its end up.

He didn't stop once to look behind to see if anyone had followed. His footsteps reverberated off rain-lashed lawyers' offices. His gaunt face reflected in windows engraved with names in gold leaf. Aquarium light shone in a lone dentist's surgery. He kept going in a southerly direction through the crashed city, slow enough to read the writing on the wall – *Cash Bingo, Hot Donuts Sweets & Rocks, Sun beds for Your Pleasure, Pillow Talk… in your Fantasy!*

Karaoke 8 till Late, Don't Beer Square, Singles Night Single Shots 99p. (Smile you're on CCTV.)

He heard hooves hitting wet streets and remembered his own horse in the stables. But he kept on walking, listening to the sound of sizzling rain in the grass verges. When the rain switched off the sky turned a deep blue. After what seemed like a lifetime he reached the dual carriageway where the car factory and the Ford axle plant were now a mosque and language school. The wind was strong and wayward, fanning his sweating skin.

Before long he was running along the three-mile beach. In the growing dark he couldn't see where the land ended and the sea began. He tried following the curve of the bay. No one was pursuing and yet he kept running, sure that he could go all night if he had to, until cover presented itself in this bay or the next, and not before.

Killing is not what it used to be. It's no big deal. People give it less thought than before. Gone were the days when the killer began an irrevocable decline in morale. Same for victims' families: they found other ways of dealing with grief besides dragging it through the courts. The new chiefs of religion helped too when they rationalised, and not before time, the concepts of heaven and hell. When the Crown Prosecution Service gave up pursuing long-range murder cases it was greeted with cheers, for freeing up man hours and resources for the police to pursue more important crimes, such as terrorism, rape and theft.

So when Pwyll returned to the town the next day he had nothing more on his mind than recovering his horse from the stables. Only by chance did he hear two stable boys talking about what had happened in Starbucks. Gwawl and his two bodyguards had slumped to the floor within seconds of each other. The serving girl, thinking they were having heart attacks, performed CPR on them (she was a second-year med student), but when the paramedics arrived they pronounced all three dead.

The serving girl had described the 'fourth man' to the police and two detectives were waiting to interview Pwyll when he returned home. But they never sought to accuse him. They were confused by the toxicology tests which discovered the vet's drug of choice in the men's bloodstream. Pwyll could offer no insight at all, and that was that. A Caesar in his own cantrefs, he was more or less above the law, providing he remained discreet. All that was required from him was a declaration of sympathy, through the media, for Gwawl and his bodyguards' families.

The story was then closed. It was down. Yet Pwyll could sleep no more. The nobility kill with impunity; that was true. It's the medieval way. But guilt is a stubborn force of nature, and democratically distributed through all creeds and class. When he asked Rhiannon for her hand in marriage he did it in such a way to allow her to refuse. He was riddled with chronic fatigue from sleep deprivation, and low self-esteem from murder.

But she didn't refuse, didn't even need a minute to consider the offer. 'Of course I'll marry you. *Duh!*' She herself was sleeping like a baby. 'You killed for my love. It's yours to take.'

Simply but forcefully she led him into her bedroom suite. No sooner inside the suite than they were inside her bed. But his performance in the sack was so terrible he fell into a narcotic sleep to escape the shame.

Morning came and he woke first. Her hair was spanned out across the pillow. Everything was warm and aromatic. In the way he used to meditate upon Alma when she slept, he now studied Rhiannon's swanlike neck, given a shifting lambency by its fine hairs, otherwise invisible except when the grain went contrary to the light. It was a moment of enduring bliss.

When she woke the spell was broken by their mutual shyness. Sleeping together made them feel more vulnerable than the sex. They used the bathroom separately and dressed quickly and without talking.

Their conversation over breakfast was cerebral and detached, telling each other about university modules they'd taken. Rhiannon studied literature and Pwyll was a geography graduate. 'Geography...'

she let out a long sigh. 'That subject used to give me vertigo in school.' Rhiannon had studied the great Walter Benjamin in her time at university, and said how weird it was that such a great intellectual like him feared, most of all, a German fairy-tale figure as the cause of all life's misfortunes. But it was all lost on Pwyll. He'd not heard of Walter Benjamin, although he did like literature in general. She asked him what he wanted to do with his life now, apart from marrying her of course, and ruling the cantrefs. But he didn't know what he wanted to do, apart from marrying her and ruling the cantrefs. He did mention though, that he'd last been happy in the army. Perhaps a professional soldier would be the thing. Then he remembered his advisors had forbidden it.

They stopped talking altogether and he started to feel irritated by the seven waitresses hovering over them, refilling his coffee cup each time he took a sip, swooping down with a table brush if he dropped as much as a crumb from his croissant. This irritation came out of a new place and he wondered if he'd ever be able to control it.

Three

After their wedding they returned to his seat to rule his cantrefs. Actually, that's not quite accurate. He didn't know how to rule, still feeding off the feel-good factor imposed on his people by Arawn... so long ago now, it seemed. Still, he did try; maintaining some of the punitive legislation set up by Arawn and clamping down on the drinking culture – after seeing what 24-hour drinking licenses did in Gwawl's cantrefs. He gave the police greater powers of arrest. There were insurgents amongst them, or so he was informed by his chief of police.

All these measures were greeted favourably until he raised income taxes to pay for them. To compensate he began taking sojourns in towns and villages to hear people's woes. This became a weekly surgery listening to pleas to send convicted perverts back to Pontyates; hearing how money was stolen each night from Gwendraeth Valley rugby club. 'How much money?' he asked. 'Twelve pound fifty; give or take...' He heard complaints about the conditions in a gun-dog farm and why something needed to be done about Denzil Davies' garage: 'It's such a mess, and so near the school as well.'

He attempted to accommodate them. But people are insatiable and the more concessions he made the more they wanted: free fuel for their wood stoves in winter; a reduction in horse taxes; free medical and dental care (you had to be kidding).

He and Rhiannon lived like many husbands and wives, with their ups and downs, the domestic routine slowly puncturing sexual desire. But they rubbed along, their relationship more or less based on entertainments: hunting and shooting parties, old films. What they didn't have was a child and that bothered others more than it bothered them. Children were messy, children were dull. But children were also heirs and Pwyll's advisors started prying

into his private affairs, making innuendos in shad-
owy corners of the house about the aristocratic
responsibility to bear sons.

His chancellor was the most persistent and finding
Pwyll alone in the library came straight out with it
– asking whether Rhiannon might be infertile.

'It could be me who's infertile,' Pwyll was hot
to reply.

His chancellor ignored that. In a roundabout way
he asked Pwyll if he ever considered taking a mistress.

What he didn't explain, to his chancellor or anyone else, is how he and Rhiannon with the help of
her pharmacist had been deliberately avoiding children. Instead, he provoked the chancellor: 'What
would you like me to do, have her executed like one
of Henry's wives?'

'Henry did divorce some of his wives.'

'I'm not divorcing Rhiannon, thank you very
much.' A log snapped in the heat of the hearth fire,
making the chancellor jump a little.

'There are tests, you know, and things you can do
as a last resort.'

'Perhaps you'd like to post a sentry outside our bedroom door? Make sure we're moaning and groaning at night.'

The chancellor smiled awkwardly and made an early exit from this consultation. Pwyll pulled out a book at random from a shelf. As chance would have it, it was called: *Thirteen Ways of Looking at the Female Nude*.

There is nothing like a slur on a woman's biological prerogative to get her back up. Pwyll shared with her his chancellor's concerns and within the month she was pregnant. After three months passed she traveled to Belgium to get a scan. When the scan confirmed the male sex of the foetus everyone in court was delighted. It was announced in towns and villages. He had no idea why they should be so happy: the nobility was about to be extended for another generation. What did that say about the ordinary man and woman in the street?

As the birth date approached, the advisors employed a maternity nurse and three nannies from Croatia to cover twenty-four hours a day, seven days a week. These women, forbidding and lugubrious, arrived at the house with one suitcase apiece and waited in the wings to take over.

When their son was born (8lb 4oz), street parties were held throughout the territory. The Croatian women stepped up and more or less took control. The only time Rhiannon saw her son in those early months was when she was breastfeeding.

Pwyll hardly got to touch the infant at all. 'If I want to see my son I have to negotiate with those dry old bitches,' he complained to his advisors.

But the advisors insisted they stay on until the boy was four years old. When Pwyll broke the news to Rhiannon she threw an ivory hair brush at the mirror in their bedroom and smashed it. 'That's thirty years bad luck,' he moaned.

He did though tell the nannies that their contracts would be terminated when their son reached his fourth birthday, and for the next three years and eleven months they succeeded in making mum and dad feel extraneous. It may have been on account of that experience that they named their son Pryderi – meaning Anxiety.

Before noon on Pryderi's fourth birthday, Pwyll fired the nannies. It afforded him the most satisfaction he'd had since killing Gwawl. He offered the women three days to pack and find new employment. Then he, Rhiannon and their son rode off the estate on bicycles.

The air was lovely at that time of year, warm and fresh ahead of a cold snap. Pwyll constructed for Pryderi a saddle on the crossbar of his bike and away they went on that piece of warmed-up Victorian technology, his son's cries and whispers intoxicating him. The cadence of pedalling was beautiful, and so was Rhiannon, who rode at his shoulder.

Soon he was pushing the bike beyond its maximum speed. A rush of grim pleasure from taking bends at speed shivered through him. He was alert to the point of strain on a hill that split the two town parks. Cycling downhill in the deepest gear, he was getting closer to the coast and the freedom he always associated with the sea.

Pwyll had his arms around the boy, enclosing him. The little boy's soft, blond hair flew around in the slipstream. He was shouting instructions to his dad, to go via the lake, chase the pigeons off the path.

Pwyll had never felt stronger. This is what it meant to be a man.

A storm had broken out the previous night and floodwater was still cannoning down the gutters. Poplars had cracked where water funnelled into dead ends. There was a faintest odour of sewerage on the wind. He flew out of the lane, shining with speed, and crossed the carriageway. He waited awhile until Rhiannon caught up then pushed the bikes over the golf links, under a tunnel beneath the defunct railway and onto the crescent-shaped beach.

In the long dune grass they hid the bikes and went on foot over the sand. They were alone on this stretch of beach. Behind their backs were rows of guest houses, pubs and a prison. The sun was hot and burning. They protected their skins with hats and with collars turned up on their shirts.

On small wooden surfboards, Pwyll gave Pryderi the ride of his life, while Rhiannon took photographs on a digital camera of them riding into shore on the white water.

This was fun and that was all it needed to be. But being a ruler, Pwyll took it upon himself to see the numinous in everything. He wanted his son to appreciate what can be achieved when you harness nature. Waves generate electrical power after all, stored in their national grid for limited domestic use. He also taught him how to survive the forces of nature. Use the waves to beat the current, was his advice in a nutshell. Ride over it and live. Fight it and drown.

All that coaching, looking back on it, was pretty self-righteous. Like many first-time parents he was trying to put the little boy together like a model kit.

Next they took him sailing on a Wayfarer dinghy. Travelling *up* the wind seemed to the boy as mysterious and exciting as defying gravity on a bike. He looked over the side into all that water with something like superstition.

They arrived the ancient way at some secluded cove and had a picnic of hazelnuts, goat's cheese, soda bread, apples and pears, home-made lemonade and cider. No meat or fish, and all locally produced. Then leaving as silently as they'd come, tacking into the wind, the warmth of the sun on their shoulders, the sea lapping against the clinker-built hull. Rhiannon continued taking digital photographs all the while.

Those were the sensational moments, carefree and full of heart.

The day following his fourth birthday, Pryderi went missing. He went missing in the middle of the night, from his bedroom. Pwyll and Rhiannon searched the big house, in every room, under every bed, inside every wardrobe and under every table. The Croatian nannies, yet to vacate the house, joined in with the search. But there was something about their behaviour that aroused Pwyll's suspicion. They weren't as desperate as they should have been, considering their former relationship with his son.

The police were called in; they dredged the ponds in the estate and the old quarry lake beyond it. Watching these figures in wetsuits and oxygen tanks swimming around the submerged fridges and washing machines, Pwyll struggled to breathe. He saw grass fields turn blood red and drums of wheat drive along the earth. He saw such things every few minutes; birds felled by hailstones dropping out of the sky.

This was divine retribution for poisoning Gwawl, no question. The gods were not dead, only sleeping. Pryderi had paid the price for murder. He did not share these thoughts with Rhiannon or anyone else.

The police interviewed everyone, including the nannies one at a time; their accounts tallied with each other. They told the police that Rhiannon had suffered severe post-natal depression for a long time after her son was born and hadn't, in their professional option, quite recovered.

Rhiannon was interviewed by a detective sergeant and a police woman for five hours, and again the next day for another four. They had to release her or charge her. So they charged her. In the absence of a body they charged her with abduction.

Abduction of children was a graver crime in people's minds than plain murder. With abduction the imagination was engaged. She might have been treated more leniently if there had been a body, if she had killed her son.

Pwyll knew his people would expect his wife to be harshly treated, or he'd have a revolt on his hands. It made him despise his subjects – who'd voted in a referendum to have the children of serial offenders removed and the vital organs of convicted terrorists harvested for transplants.

The judge, who also knew the consequences of a lenient response, deemed it appropriate that Rhiannon be publicly humiliated for failing to protect her child. He ordered her to clean toilets, cook meals and sweep yards in mental hospitals, nursing homes, rehabilitation centres and youth offenders' institutions.

Each day, Pwyll, dressed as an artisan, would go into town to meet her when she finished work. On one such evening they went to sit on a bench in a park outside the prison. Evening was beginning to fall and the leaves of ancient oak trees rustled overhead in the breeze. A botanic garden nearby released a tangy smell of lilacs into the air. Flowerbeds bordered with chains were moist with sprinkler water. Willows bent towards the stream that ran silently into a pond.

Next to the cemetery, the park is the most elegiac of places. Something about the geometrical land-scaping drew kids from off the streets, generation after generation. It was a grid for their wild play, a haven for spirits in chaos. Or where mothers brought their young children, cutting them loose to play in the glades and on the emerald lawns, secure in the knowledge they could always be found, however hard they tried to hide.

Each day after she finished work, Pwyll and Rhi-annon went looking for Pryderi. A pointless search, but one which offered some relief from despair; the only way they could bear being with one another. They were seated on the bench now, waiting for night to fall before beginning their search. She wore a baggy T shirt with long sleeves, her posture slumped.

On the tennis court two men were playing, in a manner of speaking, holding beer cans in free hands and dangling cigarettes in the mouth. The ball clipped back and forth over the net in a jovial arc. Rhiannon had been watching them intently.

'Why is it when men stay too long in one place they never grow up?' she asked. 'I bet their wives are in some coffee shop somewhere, complaining about them.'

'Did you ever complain about me in a coffee shop?'

'When would I have ever been in a coffee shop?' She sighed. 'In the days before...'

They rarely talked about what she was being made to do, in the prisons and the young offenders' institutions: he looked at her hands resting on her thighs out the corner of his eye and felt terrible shame. The skin on her hands was shredded and her fingernails bleeding.

They walked into town and immediately he felt closer to his estranged son. Illusion or not, Pryderi began to glow in his mind's eye. But it wasn't long before fleeting figures and bloodcurdling screams started to grate on his nerves. Kids were running into doors, their voices in flight. Ejected by security guards from bars and clubs they turned on one another. Kids fighting and vomiting and spilling onto the road stopped horse traffic in both directions. Bottles flying overhead had tails of frothing beer. Men in white vests were molesting girls wearing hardly anything at all, their legs streaked with fake tan. There were sirens whining from afar. It was a relief *not* to see Pryderi here.

Eight years after he'd disappeared, they stopped looking for their son.

Shortly after that, they stopped talking about him as well. When she got back each night from the penal institutions, Pwyll cooked for her the most primitive diet of eggs, potatoes, fruit and vegetables from their garden. She ate like a bird and lost half of her original weight.

They took to sleeping in separate bedrooms. Sex was dangerous. Sex was to blame for this. If he wanted to see her he would knock on her door and wait to be admitted. One time he found her sitting on the floor in her underwear looking at her image in the smoke-smeared wardrobe mirror. Tie-dyed fabrics draped over lamps cast onto the walls shades of the deep primal forest and she was all bones and right-angles, her posture terrible, back beginning to hump-up. Without make-up she looked ghoulish. Her teeth were stained and craggy. She pinched her thighs and said, 'I don't know who I am. I've got nothing left of who I used to be.'

He sometimes read to her to help her get to sleep, nineteenth-century novels out of his library. As soon as she dropped off he would pad across the landing to his own bedroom.

But he rarely slept any more. In place of sleep was repressed despair that, like carbon monoxide, put him in a trance-like state.

They had stopped searching for their son. They had stopped talking about their son. But they still allowed themselves to look at the digital photographs she'd taken of him surfing, sailing and swimming. Photos of the living are records of a specific time and place. Photos of the dead bring the dead back to life, or make the viewer feel as if he is about to join them. But photos of their son had yet another effect, in which the past seemed to reach them like light from a dead star. They would sit on a sofa in the dark with that digital camera glowing on their laps and stare at these images until the batteries ran out. For hours afterwards Pwyll could still smell the sun in Pryderi's hair.

Then that eerily quiet room would become a minefield of thought. On that sofa he'd try to picture Pryderi now, alive and well as a teenager, living with another couple. At the very worst, he pictured this couple as the type to favour astrology over astronomy, religion over science. Maybe it had been part of the divine redistribution to enable some childless couple to have a share of good fortune. He and his wife had him four years. That was something. If his only wish was for Pryderi's safety, his prayer was that he'd be enabled, educated and cultivated, loved, made to laugh, loved. Anything short of that was too tormenting to contemplate.

One Sunday, Rhiannon's only day off, they went down to the coast where those pictures were taken. They sat on the cold sand and remembered their son in silence. Soon Pwyll's memories began to take on the intensity of hallucination, and he could no longer tell for sure if he was at the seaside now or in the past. At that time of year the beach was sparsely populated with shuffling pensioners, and surfers killing time between tides. The smell of the sea was like hung game. The air was misty with spindrift, rising off surf that pounded the sand.

Pwyll stayed for hours after Rhiannon had returned to the house. He stayed until the surf calmed to nothing and the sky pressed down upon his head. Rain clouds drifting in from the west hung low and stagnant. The air was perfectly still, the sea asleep, but not dead. The pier cut into its smooth skin like a knife.

For years he used to think, if only the world was like the oceans – seminally unchanging. But now the oceans were more like the world.

On the ninth anniversary of his son's disappearance, Pwyll bought a twin-keel Kingfisher-20. As a teenager he'd learned to sail in a Kingfisher; it was in fact the only yacht he'd ever sailed. For the first few days he kept the yacht moored in the marina and slept on board. Then he decided to stay living on the boat. He'd run out of ideas on land. For the moment he let Rhiannon fare for herself.

When he took the Kingfisher out to sea for the first time the light was fading over the earth. No sooner did he leave the mainland behind than a bank of violet cloud amassed in the sky. Before him the wind hardened and his sails grew taut as skin over bone. As night fell it began to rain in sheets, blanketing the surface of the water. He brought the yacht down to storm canvas as seas lashed the deck and he heard the first crash of breaking crockery from below. On the horizon he saw merchant ships running for cover. In the wave troughs he saw nothing at all; the going was claustrophobic and dark. The storm jib spilled the wind and the canvas flopped and mooned. He strapped the tiller to go below briefly and saw leaks appearing in the coach roof and between seals in the windows. His new home was structurally insecure.

After a couple more hours and in dense blackness he saw two white flashes every five seconds, marking a munitions dump. At the buoy the sea smoked blue and yellow. A tearing ebb tide meeting the wind carved escarpments in front of his eyes. Waves stood up like brick edifices, lit from within by fiery phosphorescence.

He listened in vain for his son's voice calling to him.

This was as close as he could get to the point of no return. Sailing any further into the storm would be an act of self-destruction. He'd wanted this boat tested and he wanted himself tested. Now he bore away with the boat hard down on its rail.

A few hours later he was sailing around the mouth of the river. There was hardly a breeze this close to land, a stark contrast to the storm. He dropped the sails and went into the marina on the oars, floating past the teak schooner bricked into her own pool, like an animal caged in a zoo.

As he looked for a space to moor he could hear music leaking from the porous walls of a nightclub.

Many moons ago this marina had been implanted into the old docks with the best intentions. Traces of gantries, warehouses and coal trains had been left for aesthetic effect among energy-efficient, oxygen-producing glass office stacks. But now those office stacks were empty. The marina, once described as 'buzzing' by estate agents trying to sell high-end resi there, was just another grog-shop location. The mark of Cain appeared in the swastikas and pornographic hieroglyphics etched into the walls. Merchant ships had returned meanwhile, refitted with masts, sails and spars, and brought business back into what remained of the docks. Roaming the area once again were sailors, stevedores, fitters, lumbermen, timekeepers, Customs and Excise – and not just young men in Paul Smith shirts puking into the imprisoned sea. Children's nurseries vied for space with brothels. By day hookers moonlighted for extra cash in the nurseries.

After tying up to a pontoon he ran a hose into his water tanks. A lone fox gloved through a cobblestone alley. He dribbled a slow charge into the batteries, while checking on the safety equipment, the Decca and radar.

The yacht was still a little foreign to him. He'd yet to break it in. He poured a glass of South African red and sat down at the chart table. Charts of the British Isles lying one on top of the other he marked up with potential passages. He liked to exercise the navigational skills his father had taught him, and so many sailors had forgotten how to use. He etched in tidal and leeway vectors with a soft pencil, using dividers and protractors.

He did this mainly to distract himself.

Around midnight he took a call from Rhiannon on the ship-to-shore radio telephone. It was an odd way to communicate at the best of times. You had to wait until the speaker had finished before saying your piece. They ran their two alternating monologues for about five minutes and then gave up. He snuffed out the lamp, opened up the berth and pulled on a duvet. He lay awake in this rocking chamber for a long time before he was able to get to sleep.

The next day was Sunday and Rhiannon came

early to the marina. He was sitting in the cockpit, surveying the jagged coastline through binoculars as she appeared. She carried a large bouquet of white narcissi across her horse's neck. She dismounted and left the horse tied up where he could drink from a water trough then gingerly approached the boat along the pontoon. Pwyll relieved her of the flowers as she landed clumsily inside the cockpit. The wind blew her hair into her face.

She clambered down the companionway into the tiny cabin. 'I can't abide things that move,' she said and sat down quickly, running her hand along the light blue hopsack upholstery. 'You actually like sleeping in here?'

He was looking for something he could put the flowers in. He filled the sink and left the flowers hanging there. They sat side by side as the yacht rocked gently in the water.

'I want to talk to you, Pwyll.'

He stood up and opened the doghouse window to air the cabin. He inhaled a strong brackish scent that went to his head.

'*Frankly*, if that's all right?'

What she began to say sounded pre-composed to his ears. 'Our instinct for self-preservation's displaced when we have children by an instinct to protect them with our lives.'

He could think of nothing to add.

'When we lost Pryderi my instinct for self-preservation didn't return.'

'Meaning?'

'Meaning I don't care if I live or die.'

He didn't care to listen to her feeling sorry for herself. 'You live; we live only because he may still be alive. We stay alive for him.'

'But it's just getting harder isn't it?'

'What do you want me to say?' He began rummaging around in his cupboards.

'What are you doing?'

'Looking for something to eat.' He held up a can of haricot beans. 'Want some?'

'No thanks. Well, maybe. Sure.'

He opened the can of beans, broke open some water biscuits. He poured Paddy's whisky into two beakers, even though it was barely nine o'clock in the morning.

Through the scratched Perspex window he could see kids on bikes prowling the marina like prairie dogs. It was routine for him to watch the young, always with an eye to spotting Pryderi amongst them.

He covered water biscuits with the beans, laid the plates on the table and slid onto the seat beside her. They touched beakers. They ate and drank in silence for a while until she asked, 'What are your plans?'

'I have no plans.'

'None at all?'

'I'm ready to leave on the next tide. Beyond that, nothing.'

'And go where?'

'I don't know... out there.' He pointed towards the window, at the gathering clouds.

'You can't live on this boat forever.'

'I see no reason why not.'

'You aren't a nomad. And this isn't a proper home. It's what you escape a home in.'

'We've not had a proper home in nine years.'

'You'll be left with only yourself.'

'I already am.'

There was a strange gap opening between hearing her insights and applying them. He felt a tension in her, of someone who wouldn't be able to take her own advice.

'My love for you has always been resilient, Pwyll,' she declared. 'Despite everything.'

'Really?' He was surprised to hear this, and didn't quite believe it.

She began crying; he dared not. This situation was far too serious for displays of grief. He was doing all he could to endure, to hold steady.

He shook his head and stood up. 'I'm going sailing. Do you want to come... one word?' When she didn't answer he climbed the companionway into the cockpit.

It took him a few minutes to disconnect from the electricity supply and untie the mooring ropes. She had not left the boat, was still sitting down below. Now it was too late for her to leave. He rowed out of the marina, and as soon as he was able, raised his sails. He followed the pilotage instructions, clearing the underwater cables and sandbars just beyond the river mouth, and then altered course for an old submarine exercise area.

The tide was already changing direction in his favour. He had ten hours of flood to help push him out towards the Atlantic. As a force of habit he maximised his boat's efficiency, reducing leeway and trimming the sails. He could stay on this tack for hours now. He engaged the wind vane self-steering and went below.

He was swooning before he'd even got the whole way down the companionway. Rhiannon had vomited and the smell inside the cabin was warm and sickly sweet. She'd fallen asleep in the berth, secured by a leecloth. He took hold of her hand hanging down the side and placed it on her chest.

She opened her eyes slightly. 'My love for you may be resilient Pwyll, but it can't survive seasickness.'

'Do you want me to take you back?'

Her voice was hardly audible: 'Take me to where the palm trees grow.'

He returned to the cockpit, adjusted his course by a couple of degrees, balanced the main and genoa on a beam reach – all of which gave him a deep sense of satisfaction, a rare fleeting pleasure.

The sea is as close as you can ever come to another world.

Celtic mystics call the sea the ninth kingdom, the afterlife, the world where the dead can speak. Pwyll was convinced that if ever he was to hear his son calling to him it would be out at sea. It was just a matter of time. Our future already exists, waiting for us. Pryderi will be there waiting for us.

He listened to the sails inhale the wind, then rested his head upon the mainsheet and dissolved into the big sky, and into tiny parcels of sleep.

He woke up all anxious. He'd been dreaming vividly. A judge had asked him, 'Where are the wheels?' And he'd said, 'I honestly don't know.' 'Tell us all you know.' But he didn't know a thing and it crushed him. He racked his brain and came up empty.

For no particular reason, he altered course once

again to close haul up the NW wind, making for the southern tip of Ireland.

As they rounded the southern tip several hours later, the Atlantic stretched before him in the dark. The weather off the Irish coast was holding fine. There was a silver sheen to the sea. But as he was leaving Cape Clear he started to feel a swell running under the yacht.

He picked up a storm warning from the coastal radio station at Baltimore. A force ten was in progress two hours sail away. He had a choice of turning back or sailing into it. So he sailed into it.

No two storms are the same. Some have multiple centres of depression, some are thunder and lightning induced. None are house trained. They pay the most unexpected visits. He had no idea what this one would be like in advance. Its character would be all its own.

He began to fight big seas, where waves had reached their maximum height over a thirty-mile fetch – a composition of swells outside their area of generation and surface waves in perpetual conference. Then his Decca began letting him down, its signal weak, giving readings that he didn't believe. He had no choice but to give up trying to sail. They were lost at sea in the dark. He didn't know which way was in and which was out. He sheeted in the storm jib and lashed the tiller, locking the boat in the water, and threw the canvas sea anchor overboard. An hour before, this yacht had been a thing of life. Now it was a dead weight hanging in the sea.

Going below he found in the saloon a shambles of flung crockery and pots, like the forlorn aftermath of some marital brawl. Water in the bilges had risen to above the sole. It leaked through window seals, the cockpit lockers, ventilation and the cabin hatch. Rhiannon was lying in her own vomit. He crawled into the bunk beside her. 'Are there palm trees?' she asked softly.

She was still beautiful, except that beauty was no longer living. In that close, damp atmosphere he watched her and he watched the leaks and condensation running down the bulkheads. He monitored transmissions on the radio, listened to the lonely sound of masters' voices speaking in Russian; his unknown neighbours in an unknown place, talking to one another bridge to bridge, with the intimacy of spouses.

Not for a second did the yacht stop shaking and trembling, nor did the noise of the sea abate. He didn't know how much longer she could hold up.

Then the radio telephone began to purr. Somehow they'd picked up a signal in this white trash of a storm. Pwyll was slow to react and just stared at the black receiver for a while. He tipped himself onto the rocking cabin sole and crawled on his hands and knees to answer it. Caller and receiver cannot speak at the same time. He waited to hear the message.

'He's been found.'

'Who's been found?'

'Pryderi. Pryderi's been found.'

He climbed outside into the darkness to discover the sea crashing onto his deck like something trying to take possession. He chained himself to the cockpit by his harness and then a sheet of water hitting him in the face and chest knocked him down. He winched in the sea anchor and released the storm canvas.

The power of this storm was stunning and bold. It put the yacht under solid water almost permanently and everything became a battle to keep her afloat. The wave crests breaking were like mountains of snow. He looked up at these monsters and thought of the day when he'd taken Pryderi to the zoo. Just a toddler, he'd broken free of his pushchair, bounded away from his father, stopped at the feet of a giraffe, raised his face in amazement, and fell over backwards.

Where swell and surface waves met, the strength and height of the combined waves was the addition of each for a few seconds, before splitting apart and going in different directions, diminished in size once again. Every eight to ten minutes, two swells in a train got into step. The seventh and eleventh swell in sequence he noticed were always the highest of the group. Every twenty-third swell was twice the height of the average. This is how freak waves occur, when a wave travelling fastest in its group picks up other waves, absorbing their energy and strength. Freak waves have short lives and can expire just as quickly as a wave a third of their size. But if you are in the way at the moment of greatest strength then the odds are against you. Odds like one in twenty-three (twice the average height); one in 1,175 (thrice the average height).

He was facing chaos, while surrounded by prime, rational numbers.

Four

It was Teirnon, his former steward, who'd found their
son and had been raising him with his brother all this
time. The message he wrote Pwyll was terse to the
point of arrogance: meet us at the Little Chef on the
old A485, it said, and gave the date and time.

Pwyll and Rhiannon set off on horses in the rain.
After an hour's ride the rain shut off and the temperature soared. The wind was strong and wayward,
fanning their sweating skins. Pwyll rode slightly
behind Rhiannon watching her calves tighten and
relax. She'd dressed for the occasion in a brown skirt,
knee-high white socks and a blouse beneath her coat.
So thin, her clothes hung off her. She went contrary-
wise to desire.

They said nothing as they tied up the horses.

RUSSELL CELYN JONES

They were both struggling with what they were likely to find when they got inside the café, fearful of the moment that for so long they'd prayed would come.

He suggested they compose themselves, ready for what could be a fast-changing scene. What they mustn't be was spontaneous, say what was on their minds, or be too upset to speak. Rhiannon walked on ahead of him without a word.

They entered the café like it was water... holding their breath. The Little Chef, erstwhile hang-out for the passing motorist trade, had become a rendezvous for ex-Hells Angels who couldn't get it up anymore. Sprawled inside booths, they were listening to side two of Led Zeppelin IV on a portable CD player. Wooden prosthetics were stacked up against a Las Vegas slot machine.

As a rehearsal for when he met his son, Pwyll wondered what he must look like to these old bikers: a scrawny young-to-middle-aged man, scalloped features close to the bone. His flushed-ochre complexion was *not* a sign of good health, as his doctor explained, but of high blood pressure and the onset of diabetes.

They went to find a table by the window overlooking the road and stared out at the traffic, the rainwater flying off hooves.

The Little Chef was a burger, pie-and-custard joint, a ghetto of cholesterol to while away an hour or two. You could even smoke everywhere. It was the kind of venue where gangsters used to come in the old days to plan a bank robbery.

After they had been there seven minutes someone announced his presence with a cough. From just behind his head Pwyll heard an amicable voice say, 'This is a nice quiet corner you've found.' Pwyll looked round. Teirnon was holding a tea tray.

The boy standing just behind his right shoulder Pwyll instantly recognised. He struggled to hold a steady eye on him as blood rushed to his head and blurred his vision. Like a person seen on TV, his son seemed strangely out of reach. Yet for the next few seconds there was no one in the world but him.

His son was a wide-eyed, damp-faced teenager. He

looked down at the tray of teas Teirnon was holding, and said, 'Why didn't you get me something to eat?' These were the first words they'd heard their son speak in more than nine years.

'You want something to eat?' Teirnon sounded surprised, as if of all the things he might have expected Pryderi to say, this was not one of them.

'A custard slice or something.'

His hair was wild and snow-white from the sun. He looked like he'd just been dragged off the beach, in bare feet, ripped jeans and a T shirt with *Peacock Gym* written across the chest.

Rhiannon's head was up, eyes sparkling in the overhead strip lights. 'I'll get you something to eat. Would you like me to?'

Her voice sounded uncomfortably loud. Furrows appeared in the boy's forehead. 'Why we here?' he asked Teirnon.

'To talk,' Teirnon answered. 'Have a chat.'

'If it's the facts of life, I already know them.'

'It ain't the facts of life, don't be cheeky. Meet your next of kin. Gwri, say hello to your mother and father.'

Gwri?

After all their careful planning, the reunion was as simple as that.

'Are you called Gwri now?' Pwyll asked.

'I've thought about you every hour of every day,' Rhiannon speeded things up too fast. The emotion was flying wild like startled blackbirds from a bush.

'What's going on?' Pryderi asked Teirnon.

'I'm sorry if this is a shock...' Pwyll said and regretted it. There was nothing he could think of to say that sounded right, because there was nothing he could do to right a terrible wrong.

'I'll get you dinner,' Rhiannon persisted.

'*Cor!*' whispered Pryderi, his eyes averted. 'You're a real holy roller.'

Rhiannon mounted no explanation. She was all fallen down.

'He eats like a horse,' Teirnon explained in a manner that seemed extraordinary to Pwyll. 'Cost me and my brother an arm and a leg all these years. Hundred quid a week I reckon on food alone.'

'I can pay you that back,' Pwyll said.

'It's not the money, even though that would be good. It's the emotional cost to my brother I'm worried about. He's going to be devastated.'

'What the fuck is this?' Pryderi said.

'Language!'

Pwyll said, 'I can give you money. I can't help what your brother might feel. There was a great injustice committed here.' He looked quickly at Rhiannon, who was on the verge of tears.

'Some explanation would be good,' she said, 'for all our sakes.' She looked sternly at Teirnon. She had meant for him to start.

'Well yes,' Teirnon began, 'years after I left your employ, my brother and me started a stud farm. We kept losing the foals to horse thieves. So one night I waited to catch them with my shotgun and there was your boy, trying to steal one. He was being used by a gang, mind you. They knew we'd not kill a nipper if we caught him. They were damn right about that too. We took him in, we did.'

They were all talking as though the boy wasn't there.

'But you knew who he was?'

'On my mother's grave we did not. Only that he'd been through some trauma, we could tell that much. Some kind of abuse. In the beginning he was sullen and fighting with us all the time. Waking up screaming in the middle of the night. We didn't know who he was or where he'd come from. He never mentioned you.'

'But he's been with you for... years.' Rhiannon's voice splintered like smashed glass. 'He didn't mention us once?'

She darted a quick look at Pryderi, who was looking bored and distracted, his concerns elsewhere.

'The first moment I realised who he was, was when he'd grown up a bit. I mean, look at him. He's a dead ringer for you, my lord.' This was the first time he'd called Pwyll by his title since the days when he used to work for him. He addressed his next remark to Rhiannon. 'You've been cruelly served by a miscarriage of justice, my lady, I can say that much.'

'The nannies abducted him,' Rhiannon said. 'We never had proof, but I knew.'

'How did he end up with this gang?' Pwyll asked.

'Money passed hands,' Teirnon said simply, 'to cut-throat horse thieves with no compassion for anyone, who live short fast lives.'

'It seems we're in your debt, Teirnon,' Pwyll said.

Pryderi had had enough of being seen and not heard. 'Is that all I mean to you... a hundred quid a week?'

'Come on, ace,' Teirnon said. 'Who was it who raised you?'

This conversation between Teirnon and his prodigal son was beginning to induce in Pwyll a mild state of paranoia. It was as though he was eaves-dropping on strangers and that felt wrong somehow. It was difficult to disentangle the complex emotions. He was ashamed and indignant at the same time.

He watched as a coach arrived at the services. A refrigerated, horse-drawn truck pulled out and hit the road. A coach driver came in and took a seat, followed by several men who looked like salesmen, with women who didn't look like their wives.

'So this is my mother?' Pryderi asked Teirnon,

with his face averted. 'She's dead to me.'

'You're not dead to us,' she murmured, 'and never have been.'

'One question. Which one of you took me sailing?'

His question caught Pwyll off-guard. But he didn't have to think hard about the reply. 'Both of us did.'

Pryderi smiled just a little. 'And taught me to swim?'

'That too.'

'You mean the world to me as well,' Teirnon butted in and racked up the tension. No one wanted to appear to be fighting for the right to call this boy his own, but that was exactly what they were doing.

Pwyll and Rhiannon watched closely, far too intensely. Pryderi returned their stares with a blunt one of his own. He was struggling to digest all this information. Who could blame him? He didn't look as if he trusted his own feelings. No tears left his eyes. He blinked several times.

Then he returned to an earlier remark of Teirnon's. 'I hate it when you remind me of my financial burden to you. What could I do? I've only just left school. I went for a job and that went nowhere. It was humiliating. That was your idea as well.'

'I told him to try the building trade,' Teirnon explained. 'Get in on that racket, about the only thing that's still happening. I said "You tell them I want to go into the building trade because we're like birds with an innate ability to build nests." But he didn't know what innate means.'

'You said it means like you can't help it, you'd feel sick or something if you couldn't.'

'I never said that.'

There was a blast of 'Kashmir' in their ears from the Hells Angels' corner.

'So you've left school already?' his mother asked. 'At thirteen...'

Pryderi snorted. 'I don't go to school, that's right...' He kept darting looks at Teirnon to request some help here.

'What do you want to be then?'

'Alive... what's this, thirty questions?' He grinned at his mother and father. 'I'm not going to answer another damn thing unless I can have my lawyer present.'

Teirnon spoke up for him. 'Always things he can do without an education. He's strong as an ox. Personally, I hate students anyway.'

Teirnon was no longer obsequious. On account of having raised his son for a decade he was on an equal footing with Pwyll. He was all forward gear, his smile bolted on like one of those aliens in a horror film who inhabit human bodies on their visit to Earth. Talking of movies, he struck Pwyll like Christopher Lee in that old film *Dracula*. It was the café's overhead strip light that created the effect, throwing a shadow below his eyes and lending his receding hairline a high polish.

Pwyll twisted slightly in his seat to face his son. He was doing this repeatedly; couldn't keep his eyes off him, despite knowing better. 'Like what kind of things were you thinking about, that he could do?'

'I ain't rich,' Pryderi replied. 'I don't need money. I sleep at night, nothing wakes me up.'

'What did you like about school?'

'History.'

Personally, Pywll had no interest in the subject. History had been unkind to him for nine years. When you no longer have a family you no longer have a past. He said none of these things to his son. 'History is good...'

'Teaches us where we come from. We've been on this land thousands of years, the original Britons.'

He sheered off from his son's corrosive gaze and glimpsed a burly man in a midnight-blue suit playing the Las Vegas slot machine. He only seemed interested in the fact that it worked, and walked away before the symbols had stopped spinning in the drum. At the counter the man asked the server to get her manager. When the manager appeared in his shirtsleeves and Little Chef hat and tie, the man said loudly, 'Customs and Excise. Your gaming licence's expired.' The manager looked at him shocked but said nothing. 'I'm taking that machine away. You'll face prosecution if you don't pay the back duties within twenty-eight days.' He waved his arm out the window to two people standing next to an open-bed cart. They waved back and started to walk towards the entrance.

Led Zeppelin continued to blast away. 'Do you like this music?' Rhiannon asked her son. When she saw him flinch, she said, 'What kind of music *do* you like?'

Teirnon covered for him. 'We like that old Bruce Springsteen, don't we? The Wilfred Owen of music.'

'You can ask us questions too, if you want.'

While Pryderi paused to think of a question, Rhiannon pushed out of the seat, mumbling: 'I'm going to be sick...' she stood, recovered, then turned to Pryderi. 'Do you want a cake or something?'

'A cake, yeah, would be nice.'

As she walked away, Teirnon said in an amused manner, 'Let's hope she doesn't confuse the two things.'

'I want to go somewhere else,' Pryderi asked emphatically. But who was he asking? 'Somewhere on the peninsula.'

'What for?' Teirnon replied. 'It's all thistle and fern. Ticks everywhere. They make incisions into your flesh and give you Lyme disease.'

Pwyll was appalled. Teirnon was uncouth. He could remember all too well the horse in the living room of his brother's house and shuddered at the idea of his son being raised there. He had no right to feel indignant, but he did. He saw Rhiannon stalled at a spot equidistant from the food counter and the ladies' toilet. She seemed to waver between the two choices before shuffling towards the food counter.

Two men arrived from the car park and joined the Customs and Excise Officer at the slot machine. One was a ruddy-faced farmer, the other was actually only a teenager, in a surfing T shirt. Following instructions they unplugged the slot machine from its heavy-duty battery, leant it over on its side and carried it out of the café. As the Customs Officer held the double doors open, Pwyll saw the family resemblance with the teenager. A dad giving his son some work. It filled him with a deep sadness, at what he'd missed out on.

Rhiannon returned with a tray of pastries and cakes, she seemed to have bought the entire selection.

She placed the tray on the table and looked on as Pryderi put his fist around the lemon sponge.

Pryderi continued with that story he'd begun earlier, about his first and only job interview – how he'd caught a coach to where this company was located, rehearsing his lines, trying to make that word innate sound natural to him, when some lads came onto the coach. They were off to another postal district to duke a kid who'd pulled a shank on one of them, but didn't use it. 'That's like burying someone alive to them. It's asking for trouble. Fights are now never over. It's like another Hundred Years War.' Then these lads began to dick around with him. They pulled off his tie. If there weren't so many he'd have had a go. But instead he had to watch his tie sail out of the window. By the time of his interview he was all dishevelled. He sat down with the company director of the building firm, a Bosnian Serb. When asked why he wanted to go into the building trade, he opened his mouth to speak, and nothing came out. He couldn't even remember that word he'd been taught by Teirnon.

'I think we should go now,' Rhiannon said to Pwyll, who heard the shiver in her voice, the break-up of speech. 'It was a pleasure meeting with you.'

Pryderi answered: 'Yeah, it's been real.'

'Would you come home with us sometime?' Rhiannon asked.

'Maybe.'

Her face lit up. 'Only when you feel ready, of course.'

Pwyll stood and led the way out of the café, but was only really managing to put one foot in front of the other. They reached the horses without speaking. The clouds sparkled with trapped sunlight.

Then she crumbled and said, 'Oh, how can that be right!'

He asked, 'Do you want to come back to my boat?'

'He didn't ask about us once...'

'No,' he said softly, 'no he didn't.' He found it hard to lift his foot into the stirrup, as though his boots were made of concrete.

'He must hate me so much.'

'Hates us both.'

'I'm his mother. Fathers are meant to come and go, but mothers aren't supposed to.'

He felt deeply irritated by what she'd said. It was an enduring prejudice. Being a father was no less important or profound than being a mother. And besides, for the past nine years two men had raised their boy.

'His voice has broken, did you hear?' she said. 'He's very different from the boy we used to have.'

They rode away from the Little Chef and cut through the woods. They let their horses lead and within an hour found themselves back at the marina. She followed him on deck and down the companion-way to the saloon. In moments they were lying next to one another, without touching. Neither wished to talk about their son, scared the wrong words would tear them both to shreds.

The curtains were drawn. They lay there until darkness fell. He could hear the sound of the swollen river rushing to the sea. They were both exhausted. She began sobbing into the pillow. Not once did he offer her physical comfort. Not once did she ask for it.

She fell asleep and he listened to her breathing. He liked the sensation of having her beside him, having her asleep beside him on the bed. She was asleep for twenty-five minutes. When she woke, she must have thought she was back safely in the past with her family, for she let out a huge sigh of relief. But then she crossed her hands on her chest and pulled all the sadness up through her body.

For reasons he couldn't explain he pretended to be asleep. After a few minutes he felt the mattress expand as she got to her feet, followed by a rustle as she put on her gabardine coat.

Then something he found difficult to hide from: her warm breath as she lowered her face to kiss him on the cheek. She also knew he was feigning sleep. He had not fooled her. He listened to her climb out of the cabin up the companionway and then felt the boat rock as she crossed the deck. For some time after she'd gone he kept his eyes closed, in an attempt to fool himself.

Pwyll was relieved that their son was alive, but this was not the same as happiness. He and Rhiannon needed him back in their lives to be happy. They began to mend bridges, as a family, but it was obviously going to take time and patience. Thankfully Pryderi seemed to be a good boy. Teirnon and his brother had done a fine job. Pwyll felt resentfully grateful to them; jealous of the love their son still had for them.

Pwyll rode into the housing estate where Teirnon lived with his brother in that house that doubled as a stable, bringing with him a banker's cheque to pay off their mortgage and allow for a pension for the rest of their lives. But Teirnon would not take a penny. He said raising Pryderi was reward enough. Pwyll made it very clear that while the boy was always welcome to visit them, their tenure in *loco parentis* had come to an end.

Trying to convince Pryderi was another matter. He kept insisting on being called Gwri ('That's what my friends all know me as'), and rejected his luxurious bedroom in the huge house for a tent on the lawn. Being a teenager he was given to grunting and bouts of melancholia. But that was okay. Pwyll took some comfort in the fact that his son wasn't being polite or acting like a stranger around him.

Rhiannon asked too many questions of her son – which he didn't answer anyway. She might have done better to restrict herself, in the first instance, to cooking his favourite foods and washing his clothes, like Teirnon had done. But she couldn't cook and had never washed even her own clothes. The cooks and the maids did all that.

When she was completely out of ideas, Pwyll took him hunting in Forestry Commission land, riding on the best Arabs in the stables through the glades and along the fire-road. They both had Finnish-made Tikka T3 bolt-action rifles. They saw no deer, only an ostrich, an escapee from some local farm, its white tail bobbing up behind. The click and scratch of its claws on the gravel came as a surprise to both of them. It was dark in the woods and they could hear a high wind sobbing in the tree tops. They saw a sheep before the sheep saw them, it bolted into the woods in a real heart-attack sprint, rattling the trees, shaking the pigeons from their perches.

They were surrounded by nature, indifferent to their issues.

The sun appeared as they broke the cover of the forest and Pwyll felt its unwelcome heat on the back of his neck. Pryderi wore his Killswitch Engage pulled tightly over his sweating skull. A thin line of smoke was rising into the blueberry sky. A moment later they saw a stone bungalow. The lawn was compromised by huge boulders and flowers had been eaten to their stalks. It looked like the deer did all the gardening. Near the front door a motorcycle sat mounted on bricks, its tyres draped over the handlebars, engine in a cardboard box. A small pile of carrier bags had been pricked by foxes and a trail of chicken wings led onto the gravel.

There was something about this house that unnerved them both at the same time. It was eerie and seemed to imply things had gone wrong for the people living inside. They rode past, watchful and in silence. Pwyll was only beginning to understand how scary the countryside could be.

They stopped to eat lunch in a clearing. In the hamper the chef had packed chicken liver pâté-coated soda bread, brill tartare with soy foam and Whitstable oysters.

It was too rich for Pryderi who'd been raised on simpler fare.

His heart wasn't in the deer hunt either. 'I don't really want to kill anything,' he confessed. 'I'll eat meat but I don't want to have to kill it as well. Can we just go back?'

'Teirnon used to come on the hunts with me, back in the days...'

'It's an aristocrat thing.'

'You are an aristocrat.'

Pryderi got to his feet from the ground. 'But I wasn't raised one.'

'Is there something else you'd like us to do together?'

'Well I surf.'

'You *surf*?'

'Been surfing since I was eleven.'

'I taught you to surf.'

'Not on boards that I use now, I don't think. I've got a nine-foot Greg Noll... vintage.'

'I'll come and watch you.'

'I don't want anybody watching. If you come at all you have to come into the water.'

They began that part of their journey standing on a headland watching huge glassy swells move in grace-ful step below. A swell like that has order but comes from disorder. The source is always chaos. Waves turn up at shore like brides, wearing headsets of spindrift, but what the eye can't see is their fantastic propensity for violence.

They climbed down the cliff to the beach, Pry-deri carrying his precious Greg Noll and Pwyll with a hired board. At sea level nothing made clear sense any more. Perspective had changed. The waves looked bigger, less organised. The ground trembled with the power of dumping shore break. Pwyll's earlier excitement turned to moroseness. He looked back to where they'd been standing minutes ago on the headland, now a jumble of gun-smoked gorges and cloud-filled plateaux.

He followed his son into the water, imitating the way he launched his board. In his case the wind got underneath its rail and spun the board several times before it came back down, capsized. Cold water seeped through the neoprene of his hired wetsuit. He turned his board over, rubbed sand into the waxed deck and attached the ankle leash, as Pryderi instructed him to do, while studying their destination – an outcrop of rocks exposed by an ebbing tide. To the side of the rocks big waves were excavating over a shallow limestone reef. The swell reformed over sandbars nearer to shore and there went two ways, sweeping the bay at adjacent angles, creating a temporary channel of calmer water, a parting of the waves.

He launched himself on his board and paddled as fast as he could after Pryderi. Within seconds a great foaming wall leapt towards him. It looked light and porous, but he was soon to discover the difference. It kicked him backwards. He clung onto the board in the turbulence. When he surfaced he was back where he started. There was a whole line of these burly waves to negotiate and they made him think of people who'd scared him: Arawn. Havgan. Gwawl. He set off again, made twenty metres and lost fifteen.

Ploughing on, getting creamed, surfacing, ploughing on – until he reached a clean face. He pushed the nose of the board through its lip and skidded down the backside, into a light that was pink and misty with vapour. The wave shivered and cracked as it gave into gravity. Now clear of the sandbars they altered course for the reef.

They circled in behind the rocks where the line was purest. If the waves seemed quiet from the headland, they were not quiet here. The noise they made breaking over the reef sounded like quarry explosions. The sea clicked, rattled and fizzed. The exposed outcrop of rocks was covered with sharp mussel and whelk shells. A place so obviously to be avoided was irresistible to surfers.

There was a conflict of tensions between the

ever-moving sea and the reef rooted to the ground. Negotiating between those two elements is what Pryderi aimed to do. There was no sweeter joy for him than riding a three-metre wave out of trouble. So why did he spend thirty minutes turning in the gyre of cross-currents without tackling a single one? He was scared. He was respectful. He was just thirteen years old.

An irregularity on the horizon gave due notice of ructions soon to come. A set of three waves banked around the point. There were always three waves in a set, each one larger than its predecessor. They let the first one go, to be greeted with the second of the set, feathering at the lip, shivering on the brink of collapse.

The third wave would be closed out. Pryderi shouted over the noise of surf: 'We have to go *now*!'

Pwyll had no intention of riding a wave just yet and paddled over to the safety of the channel. From there he watched Pryderi slip his weight to the back of the board, spin round, fall across the deck, and stroke towards the exposed rocks. On the rocks were

crabs creeping out from behind fringes of weed,
clawing at the air. The water beneath Pryderi began
to drain, sucked up into the wave behind him. His
arms tangled in kelp as the stern lifted and he began
to accelerate. He got to his feet in one move,
crouching to lower his centre of gravity. He had put
himself in maximum danger, taking off in front of
the rock. He dropped down into the trough and
turned into the unbroken face of the wave. He rode
a sheet of smoked glass, scored with kelp and streaked
with foam. In the deep hollow he began to react
intuitively to what the wave was doing, to its schedule of collapsing power. The board, shaking and
flapping in front of him, pushed back hard against
the balls of his feet. The lip of the wave snapped,
curled and put a roof over his head. He sped through
a tunnel with a curtain of foam lifted off the wall
by the exhaust of the breaking section. The tunnel
collapsing at one end was building at the other, and
filled with imprisoned sunlight. His face was close to
its face. Pwyll heard two distinct sounds: the wave
disembowelling itself on the reef and the sizzling of

a million air bubbles like bees in a hive. And then Pryderi was gone, the wave hid him from sight.

Pwyll was full of consternation for the son he could no longer see.

The ride lasted no more than twenty seconds. Pryderi quit the wave, kicked out the back and yelped. His ecstasy was infectious. Pwyll was stoked too, his heart pumping blood round his arteries.

So much sudden happiness disorientated Pwyll and he got caught inside. The first wave of a trinity lifted him skywards and seconds later drenched him in a twenty-foot veil of spray. The wave took its scheduled fairground ride over the rocks. Pieces of limestone flew off into the air. He tried scrambling away into the safety of the channel but got caught by the second wave that ripped the board from his grasp. The following seconds were unbearable ones. The wave wouldn't let him up. The turbulence of tons of collapsing water buffeted him. There was nothing he could do except journey at its discretion and preserve oxygen as best he could. The violence above matched the pain in his torn limbs and sobbing muscles. He sank deeper into ever-darkening folds of cold water. He didn't know the bottom from the top. He was bounced against the rock bottom and the oxygen went in an instant.

When he surfaced there were spectrums in his eyes, water pouring out of every orifice in his head. His board lay on the surface nearby, still attached to his ankle by the leash. As he climbed back on he saw his son scratch for a wave and make an entry so far left to seem reckless. But what he did from the moment he was up he'd never seen any man or boy do. The ride was more than an escape from dangerous elements, it was a conquest. He transformed a force of nature into a subservient force of nature.

They met again at the line-out. Pryderi shouted at his father, his voice sounding like beaten tin. 'Are you okay?'

'Yes!' The wind spun and threw his reply into the air.

'I saw you get caught.' Pryderi was smiling. 'I was worried for a moment.'

These were the glory days, being with his son.

RUSSELL CELYN JONES

'Are you ever going to catch a wave?'

'I'm fine...' Pwyll gave him the thumbs-up sign. 'Enjoying myself.'

They fought the rip together, shuttling around to stay in position. Then two other surfers joined them in the line-out. They were older than Pryderi by some years but he was familiar with them, as familiar as kin it seemed. One was Scottish, the other Irish and both called him Gwri.

'This is my father,' Pryderi introduced him, and the word sent a shiver down Pwyll's spine. It was a title he'd not heard in a long time and the one he cherished far more than Lord.

While the two surfers went for a take-off, Pryderi explained to his father how those guys lived in summer chalets during the winter, keeping the chill off at night with charity-shop blankets. They raided fields at dawn to purloin fruit and vegetables, whatever was in season, and stole the odd scrawny chicken to cook over a driftwood fire. They teased crabs out from behind fringes of weed and line-fished off the rocks. 'There's a lot of them, yeah, living on the

156

edge, cut off from family, some evading the law or dodging the draft.'

Pwyll heard the enchantment in his voice and was shocked. He'd never heard anyone speak so highly of a crowd who had so little. This was a glamour he did not understand. Finally he said, 'Surfing is a Celtic thing, is it not?'

'Because surf's on the west coast, mainly,' Pryderi said, then added in a dreamy voice, 'One day I want to surf in California. Live in permanent sunshine. Never see a single blemish in the sky. Guys sleep in wrecked cars, caravans with no roofs, living off fruit from the trees. In southern California they got olives, lemons, oranges growing wild.'

Pwyll was deflated to hear him talk like that, about the lure of other pastures. He was scared he might leave, just when he'd found him.

They had no more time to dwell on this as a set was coming in, thrusting them back into the moment. Pwyll waited this one out, and watched Pryderi skid down a wave. After he'd passed by he saw his head pop up over the back, disappear, pop up again and then he went airborne kicking out for good, with a second to spare before the wave dumped onto the rocks.

They stayed in the water for hours. Evening began to fall and the waves made purple forms against a blood-red sky. Cormorants slid by, skimming the surface of the sea. The tide had gone past its lowest ebb and was creeping back over the reef. The wind slackened and the sea gained some moderation. Although less hollow, the waves were exhilarating in a different way, spectral and enigmatic.

Pwyll began to understand more about his son in those hours. The sea was his territory, where he rode away from his troubles. He had his woes but got everything in perspective out here. Heavy water scoured the difficult emotions. In the smoke and unreason of the surf he was content.

From time to time, Pryderi expressed opinions – about such things as crimes and barbarities committed in the name of the Moroccans being no different to the crimes and barbarities committed throughout history in the name of the best intentions. Like the

Dutch Reformed Church leaders of South Africa who built the Apartheid state. Or the American Christian parents who sacrificed thousands of teenagers in Vietnam and Iraq; all for a doctrine that promised freedom with compassion.

He didn't learn these things at school. It was the opinions of the two older surfers streaking past on the same wave that Pwyll could hear in Pryderi's voice. Such footwork geniuses could only be right about history, apparently. These gladiators of the sea his son had apprenticed himself to reminded Pwyll strongly of the men he'd met in the military. But his son wasn't commanding them. He was their equal, had become classless in a way Pwyll had failed to do in his short stint in the army. It was an admirable state of affairs for someone born into privilege. Only by being plucked from that privileged world could this be done.

Pryderi took another wave. A liquid roof enclosed him as he carved into the shoulder. He shifted his back foot to the left gunwale and cut back into the turbine, the nerve centre. He was heading for the rock, about to lasso himself in the kelp. A one-eighty degree turn brought him round again and a second roof formed over his head. As the wave was about to collapse down its entire length he cut out the back. As he was paddling back out, the blueprint of that wave filed itself away in Pwyll's head. The other waves his son had ridden were all there, each one different, like intense characters briefly encountered. Like the human face, no two waves were exactly alike.

Over the next hour Pryderi surfed less. He was getting tired. Pwyll chose this moment to ask the question that had been burning inside him for weeks. 'Can you remember much about the people who abducted you?'

'A little. Some.'

'Who were they?'

'People I wouldn't pull out of a burning house even if I was in a fireman's suit.'

'What did they do to you?'

'I don't want to talk about it,' he said with such anger, Pwyll knew he'd pushed it too far too soon.

Now his son trembled with emotion. He seemed to be living back in the troubled past. With his head in such a place he shouldn't have gone for another ride. The insecure structure approaching seemed to be just too much to cope with.

It was an avalanche of trouble, but Pryderi turned his board to go. His take-off was late. Tons of water followed him down the face where he turned too fast in response to desperate conditions. Pwyll saw his fin pop out. The board spun, returned him back up the face to meet head-on the sheet of free-falling water.

Then he was gone, sucked up into the grinding wave. Pwyll stretched his torso to see where he was. He was holding his own breath until he saw him reappear – on the rock, bounced there by the wave. Water was draining off to each side. His board had gone, the leash snapped. His wetsuit jacket had gone, ripped off his back. Blood was streaking down his head. Pryderi snatched clumps of kelp as the next wave came down upon him with a long whistling howl. Then he was underwater again. The water drained off the rock and he was there still, fighting to release the kelp entangled around his foot. The third wave in the set approached at twenty miles an hour, trembling in anticipation of its little human snack.

The third wave hit, its waters poured down each side of the rock. And Pwyll could no longer see his son... anywhere.

He circled the area feeling absolutely desperate. Seconds tolled by. Then he spotted him thirty metres away, floating on his back, with nothing left to give, drifting on the swell. Time seemed to own him as the current swept him further out to sea. Pwyll fell across the deck of his board and paddled with all he'd got. He kept losing sight of his son behind steep walls of incoming waves. These were the terrible moments. His mind was too far ahead of his body, telling Pryderi to hang on in.

When he got to him his son was almost gone. He slipped a hand under the neck and lifted his son's head onto the glass deck. There was blood in the water. Pryderi hung weakly to his father's wrists. Pwyll began the long haul into shore, through the fierce rip and the rolling waves.

The sea is a wilderness that makes no judgments. It has an ego that never overwhelms with its love. However violent the waves, they will always deliver you safely onto shore.

Rhiannon wanted to take Pryderi shopping for new clothes. It seemed easier than washing the old ones. Pryderi shrugged. He didn't care one way or another. He was still wary of his parents. He was a teenager who'd not seen sight of them in nine years, what could you expect? As a rule, teenagers rarely see their parents as people with rich lives and emotions. They are more symbolic than real. But in Pryderi's case his parents were entirely symbolic.

He trailed behind them into an aisle of casual wear. But when his mother said, 'You have to go back to school, you know,' he was set to walk straight out of the store.

Pwyll read the situation just in time. 'Perhaps you could skip school and go straight into politics.'

'That's not funny, Pwyll,' Rhiannon said.

Pryderi scraped several pairs of jeans and T shirts off the racks and sauntered into the changing rooms. Pwyll and Rhiannon stood staring mesmerised at his changing room. His bare ankles and feet sheathed in white socks were visible in the space below the door.

Rhiannon said, dreamily, 'How things turn out, you can never predict... are you happy?' She looked into his eyes.

'I'm getting there.'

Pryderi came out of the changing room wearing a new, oversized T shirt and black jeans, with the other garments draped over his arm.

'I heard you two talking,' he said.

'It was nothing,' Rhiannon replied.

'Are you going to lie to me now?'

Pwyll and Rhiannon looked at each other in panic.

Pwyll said, 'I killed a man. Is that honest enough for you?'

'You killed a man?' Pryderi sounded impressed.

'Yes, I suppose I did. More than one.'

Rhiannon said, 'He did it for me. He did it for love.'

'Let me get this straight. My parents are like the Macbeth family?'

'I'd kill for you too, Pryderi, if I had to.'

For some reason Pryderi found this amusing and laughed all the way to the cashier.

As they were leaving with their purchases in carrier bags, clouds changed course in the sky. Rain falling over the sea came rattling into town. They walked to where they had left the horses, in an industrial zone long ago disabled. Abandoned factories and soon-to-be demolished rows of terraced houses studded the ground. Gas containers rusted in the salty air. Electricity pylons looming overhead had lost most of their wires, dangling down like broken guitar strings.

At the heart of everything was a druidic stone circle. Around the stones a crowd had gathered. Banners in the wind bore the words: *Save our sons and daughters*. Someone dressed all in black shouted through a megaphone: 'We know the devil isn't walking around here with a pitchfork and horns. He's in these gangs slaying our children.'

Pwyll had always felt detached from such protests, from grass-roots politics, but showed an interest now. With his son at his side he felt moved by these parents in mourning. Their children would *not* be coming back. He recalled something Pryderi had said about fights between teenagers never ending, like another Hundred Years War.

They retrieved their horses down by the canal. Long out of use, the canal was full of lilies. A derelict barge, partially sunk, was housing a family of swans that were swimming in and out of the cabin – cygnets on the back of the pen. There was an old billboard for New Era Diesel and an advertisement for Telford Homes, who decades ago began renovating the warehouses on the canal before they had to abandon the project. Their plant equipment lay broken, like the Hymac steam dredger plunged head down into the water.

As they were preparing to mount up, a crowd of young riders appeared on bikes. Pwyll could see the tension in their shoulders, in their straight arms welded onto handlebars. These were not nice boys.

He saw something else: Pryderi agitated to the point of breakdown.

'What's the matter?' Pwyll asked. 'Do you know them?'

'Guys like that ran my life for a long time.'

Someone amongst the demonstrators recognised the noble family in their midst. Word passed round like a rumour of goodwill and a parting was made into the druidic stone circle. They wanted Lord Pwyll to speak to them.

Pwyll didn't know how to react. He grew cold all over as they waited for him to say something reassuring. He turned to Pryderi. 'I don't know what to say to them.'

Pryderi shook his head in exasperation then slid off his saddle to the ground. He gave his mother his reins and walked into the crowd. Now even the cyclists were curious, as he began to climb on top of the largest stone. He stood there for a moment, above the heads of the crowd.

Someone shouted, 'Who are you?'

Pryderi took a moment to compose himself. And

in that moment Pwyll glimpsed the veronica of his son's soul.

'I am Pryderi, son of Lord Pwyll,' he shouted back to the crowd, 'and this is what you must do.'

The First Branch of the *Mabinogion*
Pwyll, Lord of Dyfed

The young Lord Pwyll of Dyfed is out hunting when he offends Arawn, king of Annwfn, the Celtic Otherworld.

To repay the insult, Arawn tells Pwyll he must swap places and appearances with him for a year, and make peace with a troublesome neighbouring king, Hafgan. This includes sharing a bed with Arawn's wife, which Pwyll does without touching her. At the end of the year the two men meet and find they have done well in each other's place.

Feasting at his court in Arberth, Pwyll sees a beautiful woman riding by. He cannot catch her, but eventually he asks her to stop and she does. Her name is Rhiannon and she tells him she loves him but has to marry another man, Gwawl. Pwyll agrees to free her from Gwawl, but is at first outwitted by him before catching him in an enchanted food bag. Pwyll and Rhiannon are married and eventually have a son, Pryderi. But the infant Pryderi disappears and his nurses blame Rhiannon, who is publicly punished.

Teyrnon, lord of Gwent Is Coed, is battling to stop the theft of foals, bringing his horse into his house to protect it. One night as he fights the thief he finds a child wrapped in silk, whom he and his wife take in and bring up as their own. They call him Gwri.

The boy grows strong and handsome and, after some years, the couple hear about Rhiannon's loss and punishment and recognise Gwri as Pwyll's son, Pryderi.

They return him, asking for no reward, and Pryderi goes on to become a great ruler.

A brief synopsis: for the full story of the First Branch see
The Mabinogion, A new translation by Sioned Davies
(Oxford World's Classics, 2007)

Afterword

The stories collected in the *Mabinogion* are like a
prose version of ancient Greek drama, in that most
of the action is set off-stage, rather than on it. The
landscapes of Wales are barely described. Themes
alluded to, such as identity, chivalry, the supernatural,
are never more than speculative. Randomly calami-
tous or magical events that create social and political
upheaval are undramatically rendered. The medieval,
oral, storytelling tradition has not kept pace with
the modern world and no longer engages the contemporary reader. As a result, one of the world's
oldest and most revered texts is only ever studied
now in schools and universities.

The commission by Seren to rewrite any one of the
stories (or branches) was an irresistible opportunity

to revive a dead art in entirely my own way. I first read the *Mabinogion* as a schoolboy in Swansea, and would describe my experience as reluctant. I re-read it again in my university days and enjoyed it a little more. Returning to it as a writer I felt I was attending unfinished business. The *Mabinogion* has never undergone a modernising adaptation of any kind, despite W.B. Yeats urging in 1879 that 'every new fountain of legends is a new intoxication for the imagination of the world'.

My intention was to re-interpret antiquity from a modern perspective, to replenish this rather arid story with a post-Freudian, post-feminist vitality. With religious wars, piracy on the high seas, global plagues on the ascendancy it is not too difficult to imagine a fully medieval world becoming our destiny, so I set my version in the near future. I have reconstituted the first story of the *Mabinogion*, 'Pwyll Lord of Dyfed', in line with modern fictional techniques: made psychological what was magical, realistic what was whimsical. The structural shape of the story had to change to accomplish these ambitions, but this seems apposite bearing in mind the *Mabinogion* is the work of multiple authors that evolved over a span of centuries.

The original narrative work juxtaposes the mundane with the magical, the private with the public. Characters are courtly and refined, the product of an early Christian society in a predominantly pagan world. There are references to power struggles in the court and political in-fighting, the experience of women in violent society, sex and childbirth. Set in south-west Wales, geographically close to where the Underworld was deemed to be, it introduces Rhiannon the 'Great Queen' who has magical powers over horses and birds. Pwyll undergoes a series of trials before he can rule his kingdom of Dyfed and become this Queen's consort. Their child is the future hero, Pryderi, whose disappearance in infancy and reappearance several years later is where this branch ends.

There is so much packed so tightly into this story it was hard to 'see' anything; like a treatment for a work yet to be fully realised. My novella necessarily became a five-fold expansion and amplification of the original story. Some of the themes deeply embedded in the medieval branch, once got at, tapped into my preoccupations as a novelist. I was keen to bring to life the rivalry between men, codes of behaviour separating genders, experience of war, the enterprise of marriage and children and the rites of passage of boys into manhood. I have never written about aristocracy before and the model I kept in mind for the young Lord Pwyll was our current Prince Harry. His reputation as a hellraiser, night-clubbing and drinking his youth away, and the rather staged attempt to show the world his manliness with the British Armed Forces in Afghanistan, is redolent of Shakespeare's *Henry IV*.

Another specific interest for me, and a theme with striking contemporary resonances, was the disappearance of Pwyll and Rhiannon's son. I wanted to explore how such a traumatic event would impact upon a marriage. Living with such a loss and then dealing with the child's return seems to me to be an equally true test of manhood. Other things that appealed from the original were its potentially strong female characters, imaginative possibilities for narrative and the fact that it is confined to the South Wales of my childhood. I had fun writing it and hope that experience extends to the reader.

Russell Celyn Jones

Acknowledgements

Thanks are due to Professor Helen Fulton for her creative interpretations of the *Mabinogion*; Eoin and Kathy Monks for the use of their shed in Wicklow, Ireland, where much of this book was written, and for weeks of hospitality; and to Aoife, for the love.